The Deepest Burn

The Deepest Burn
A Novel by- Kristen Tru

Dedicated to
Judy Salas for always inspiring me to be myself without fear.

Cover by Richard Ingersoll

Who Set the Boy on Fire?

All adventures begin with a single door. One that looks just like any other door, which makes it difficult to find. And then, once you find one, the most special of doors are also the most difficult to open.

For one girl in a small town in Colorado, a doorknob was turning.

She was, of course, completely unaware. Only I could see the ominous shift in the surrounding air. If she had been aware then, perhaps she wouldn't have been preparing for her very first date. But instead, blissfully ignorant of the looming consequences, she was curling her hair. While she curled a crucial chocolate-brown strand near the front, she began stressing over whether she looked ugly in the green dress with the lace her pa helped her choose for the evening. This panic clouded her mind so much that only the disturbing stink of burning hair reminded her to release her trapped hair.

She pulled the burnt piece of hair behind her ear and tried on the tight dress. She twirled around a few times in front of her mirror that hung on her door. Once she felt confident that she didn't look bad in it, she started to worry that maybe she was overdressed. Once she decided she wasn't overdressed, she worried that maybe she was underdressed. And then, of course, she worried that she was curling her hair too tightly, or too loosely, and that her makeup was too much, and that her nail polish clashed, and a hundred and one other things that could possibly go wrong.

I never have these kinds of problems.

Emery was a pretty girl, although she would never believe that. When she looked in the mirror, she didn't see her silky, rich brown hair or her hazel eyes that looked brown unless you were fortunate enough to get close enough to see the flecks of gold in them, and only one person ever would. No, instead, she saw someone entirely different, some warped version of herself. She looked closer in the mirror and tried to tell herself that other people thought she was pretty, but the thought made her laugh out loud and look away.

Despite her perception of shortcomings, one of the cutest boys at her school, Levi, had recently asked her on a date. Levi had secretly thought Emery was cute since they were in Elementary School, but until someone else said she was cute as well, he wouldn't have dared to say anything about it. But recently, during a sleepover, some other boys and theys had dared him to ask Emery out, and he quietly rejoiced in the alignment between his desires and his friends'.

Across town, Levi was also preparing at his own home, with a good nap, sprawled out across his bed and drooling onto his dirty pillow. At the same time, Emery put the finishing touches on her hair and changed into a little black dress that she thought was a safer bet. She walked downstairs slowly, as if her parents might be waiting for her as they always did in the movies that she loved so dearly.

They weren't.

But she still tried to enjoy the moment. She would be sixteen in two weeks, but she had never been asked to a dance or even on a date before. So, she tried to take in the moment and even told herself that this was the beginning for her. All good things would begin coming her way. The unfortunate irony is that it was the beginning for her, just not the one she was hoping for.

The problem with beginnings is that the word carries hope while the reality rarely accompanies it.

Emery sat on the sunken-in floral couch in their living room and took her phone out of her pink mini-backpack to look at the time.

7:05 pm.

He was only 5 minutes late. He was probably trying to be a little late because cool kids were always late.

Across town, Levi was still napping. He was completely sprawled out now, like a relaxed dog across his old astronaut sheets that were still on his bed, even though he had long since outgrown them.

Emery looked through the same Facebook feed that she had already looked at twice, begging someone to post again so that she could pretend to be doing something a bit more effectively. But she couldn't help but look at the time.

7:20.

That couldn't be normal. She went back and forth about ten times between whether or not she should text Levi. Eventually, almost as if her fingers took over while her brain screamed no, she texted him.

Hey!

Poor girl. That text would haunt Emery night after night. It seemed that every time she tried to fall asleep, this was ritually in her brain from here on out. Why couldn't she have more pride and not texted him at all when he hadn't shown up? She would wonder if that text, just something about it, made Levi decide not to come. Maybe it was too harsh? Too casual? Maybe she shouldn't have a phone at all. She once decided teens should have to pass a test showing they had the discipline to not send texts that would embarrass them later in life.

8:00 pm.

Emery finally gave up. She knew that Levi wasn't coming. Ironically, at around the same time, Levi woke up. He knew immediately what he had done and felt terrible when he saw the text from Emery on his phone. But as is the case with many teenagers, he simply was not in possession of the emotional intelligence required to be honest with Emery. He assumed she probably thought he was some jerk that blew her off, and he simply thought it was easier to be some jerk than to be honest and risk rejection.

Emery determined after a couple quiet tears into a faded couch pillow that she would leave the house, regardless. She deserved to still have someone see the work she'd put into getting ready. She grabbed a gray hoodie to look more casual and walked out of the house towards a local bowling alley that was a few blocks away.

The bowling alley, much to its dismay, was the hangout for high schoolers from every local school. She knew that kids from her school would be there. She thought to herself on the walk over that maybe she would get asked on a date by someone else at the alley and fall madly in love. Maybe this was actually the new beginning.

It was only a ten-minute walk, and when she could finally see the alley, she got quickly nervous about going at all. She started practicing out loud what she would say to people when she got there.

"Hey, what's up?"

"No, I didn't have a date tonight."

"Hey, how are you? Can I play too?"

"Hiiiii, guys bowling."

They were just getting worse as the bowling alley inched closer and closer. She'd better stop. She'd better just go home, she thought. Then she found the bowling alley in full view in front of her, with possibilities, good or bad now within complete reach. She finally agreed as she stood in front of it that she would just go inside, and whatever happened would happen.

Unfortunately, she didn't commit, and instead she stood and stared at the building for a long while. It was an old, cement gray building with large, blue-striped bowling pins lined in front of it all the way around. The gigantic neon sign that said AL's BOWLING at the top never lit up, and she found herself in that moment, wondering why. Maybe they didn't have the money, and the owners argued over whether they should replace the light or pay the teenage cashier. Maybe there wasn't anyone in town qualified to fix it. Maybe the owners just didn't care.

Then as if her light went out as well, she suddenly thought of how she had gotten to this very moment. Tonight, was supposed to be her first date. It was supposed to be the night that she thought back on and remembered fondly, maybe the first of many dates. Yet, instead of analyzing the details of Levi's face as she should have been, she was analyzing the subtle details of the bowling alley that she had seen a thousand times before. She shook her head at her sorrow, which was always hiding near these exciting moments in her life.

On the other hand, Levi's night had taken a decidedly different turn. After he committed to standing Emery up, he was not feeling great about himself. This was not the first time that Levi acted like this. He would never admit it, but it was the same behavior he had observed from his father so many times. A deep fear of disappointment or embarrassment, to the point he hurt others at all costs to avoid losing himself. But Levi did not like the feeling it gave him in his gut, the guilt just sitting under his skin.

So, he gelled back his blonde hair and threw on some blue jeans and his hockey t-shirt. He knew that if he stayed home, he would continue to feel guilty, so he made his way to the bowling alley, where he was sure he could see some friends.

I can't tell you why Emery didn't think about whether Levi could be at the bowling alley. One of Emery's many woeful attributes is her ability to let things like this slip through the cracks. She spent so much time thinking about so many possible outcomes and issues that she had no time for thinking about the most realistic outcomes and certainly no time to prepare for them. Her mind simply wouldn't slow down enough for her to see them. So, unfortunately, as she gathered the guts to enter the establishment, Levi had gathered the guts to kiss Eva Lucero in the front of the bowling alley on a pool table.

Eva Lucero and Emery had been enemies since they were children. It feels dramatic to be enemies as children, but to them it felt like an understatement. Everything Emery did, Eva did with a bit more flash. At the very beginning of their relationship, Emery had told Eva she would be a vampire for Halloween. Emery showed up to school the next day with plastic white teeth and a shiny new red cape. Eva walked into the room with a professionally made vampire costume, complete with white contacts, a red curly wig, and teeth that dripped fake blood. Emery took her fake fangs out throughout the day, then threw her cape in the trash at lunch and told everyone she talked to how dumb Halloween was. Another time Eva told Emery she would never be a real Mexican since she was adopted, even though one of her dads was also Mexican and had brought her up learning about her culture.

Emery didn't think about any of those things when she saw Eva sitting on the pool table to the right of the entrance and making out with Levi. No, Emery didn't remember anything she hated or liked about either of them—because before she knew it, there was only fire, the table lit up so fast she couldn't even see where it came from. She froze for a moment, staring as people ran by her, yelling "FIRE!" and pushed her out of the way.

It only took a moment for their screams to break through her confusion, and Emery bolted forward as she tore off her hoodie and tried to stamp out the flames spreading over Eva's body. But it just kept spreading and spreading, and started traveling up Emery's right arm—

With the speed of a blink, she looked down and her arm was completely on fire, then in another blink, it was gone. She ran over to the bar on the side and looked for water, but by the time she turned around, the fire had grown, and she could no longer get back to Eva and Levi. Emery paused and looked around the alley to see if other people were also in distress or if her only option was to kill herself trying to save the two people she hated most in the world. There wasn't anyone else—but there was a pair of large glass doors in front of the alley. They were still intact and almost begged for her to run through them to safety before it was too late.

She looked back to the evil couple. Levi rolled back and forth on the ground, and Eva was seemingly stripping off her clothes that were still ablaze. All while flames seemed to completely circle them now. They wouldn't be able to make it to the door, even if Emery continued trying to help them. Unless they could escape the flames themselves, there wasn't a way for them to move.

Emery could have, at this point, easily left the building. She could have been seen as a hero for staying behind in the first place to try to help Levi and Eva. It seemed every other kid and adult had run for their lives already, the realistic response to a massive fire.

That door only meant one thing: safety. Both hers and theirs. Could she run into the fire and try running out with them? If she wanted to come out of this alive, they needed a barrier. She gathered towels from around the bar and started throwing them in a sink as she let the water run. The plan itself was incredibly flawed. The water-soaked towels would be no match for the flames coming after them, and she knew it.

So, when a pair of arms, dressed in rough cloth, wrapped around her to carry her out of the building, there was no denying Emery's relief. But the relief was replaced with a pain of the knowledge that she had failed and could do no more to help. Even though she hated Eva, and Levi too right now, that didn't mean she wanted them to die. She didn't want anyone to die.

The firefighter carried her to the parking lot, where everyone who'd already gotten out was standing and watching and he set her down next to an ambulance. She didn't answer when he tried to ask if she was okay, merely stared at the burning building, and the firefighter only had a moment to spare before he was needed back on the scene.

"Emery, are you ok? Emery, can you hear me?" A familiar voice drifted into her awareness, but Emery could not tear her gaze away from the fire. She recognized the voice as a friend from school, but she was frozen. Her breath held in purgatory as the unlit neon sign slowly creaked and swayed, the fixings snapping one by one until it ultimately crashed into the flames below it. Her chest grew tight, her lungs burning, but still she could not breathe, not until she watched the fire-fighters first walk Eva out, followed by one carrying Levi—and then she exhaled.

"I'm fine, Jose," she murmured. "Just a couple of small burns and lots of ash, it looks worse than it is." She had been on fire, she knew that, so she had to be burned somewhere—but she couldn't feel it. There was no pain emanating from her arm; no pain at all. But she didn't have the time, nor the concern to deal with that, and had she given them the chance before she ran, she would have told the paramedics and the police just that.

But she did not give them the chance, and instead she ran as fast as she could in the direction of home. Her lungs burned from the effort and her eyes stung; tears spilled over and ran down her cheeks, and she tried to tell herself it was only because of the ash in her eyes, even though deep down she knew that wasn't true at all.

When Emery arrived home, she was disappointed to see her parents' red little car out front. They thought she was on a date, and instead, she was returning looking like she had just survived a fire, which is exactly what had happened—and she had no idea how to explain that to them. So, she ran through the door and upstairs to the bathroom so quickly that I wondered whether she should have joined the track team and whether something small like that would have changed her fate.

She shed her clothes slowly and gingerly entered the shower. There was a small burn on her left arm, and smaller burns still on her shoulders that only smoldered more with the hot water. She eventually lowered herself to sit on the shower floor and as she wondered desperately how her evening had gone from preparing for her first date to a bowling alley fire. Her thoughts definitely drifted to Eva and Levi, who had to be badly hurt, and she decided she would call the hospital to check on them, either tonight or in the morning. She also hoped the bowling alley survived somehow and started to think of how the town could fundraise to rebuild it.

A knock came at the door once she got out of the shower and changed into clean, ash-free clothes. It made her think about how her pa always knew exactly when he could finally come to bother her. On the other hand, her dad was less likely to come to check immediately, not because he didn't care, but because her pa was always much faster and usually more panicked at dealing with any situation. Emery's pa, Erick, was actually a very kind father, although not the smartest—but he was not so dumb that he would not notice his daughter came home smelling terribly like smoke, covered in ash, and running through the house as fast as a flame.

"Emery, it's pa," he said like Emery might have thought her door led to the outside, secret world and not their home.

"Come in." she said, wiping a lingering tear just in time.

Erick walked in and looked around the room like he would find the fire he was smelling in there before he took a seat on Emery's bed. He put his long dark hair in a bun as he spoke, much like Emery's own.

"What happened, Emery?" He said putting his arm around her shoulder carefully as if he was deactivating a bomb.

"There was a fire at the bowling alley." She said, getting off the bed and moving to her mirror.

"Are you ok?" he said calmly, trying not to make her shut completely down.

Emery looked in the mirror as she braided her wet hair, unable to meet his eyes. "Fine, Pa."

"Is your date...ok?"

Then Emery thought of her date once more, she knew it was the one thing she had been trying to avoid at all costs. But it was too late now, she didn't just think about it. She felt it all over again. She pictured Eva and Levi kissing, right there, on what was supposed to be her first date.

"Pa, I don't really want to talk about it right now."

Erick took this as his cue and started to leave the room. But once he reached the door, he turned back for a moment, hesitating.

"Let me know when you are ready to talk, we are here."

She nodded, not looking at him. Once the door shut, she shed her clothes. She got back into the shower and turned the water back on. She needed space to think. She needed space to cry.

Emery spent the rest of the shower letting her tears blend with the water.

I regret that so far; I have had only bad news to tell you— and I haven't even revealed the terrible events that will happen to Levi after this. But I will give you good news, to soften the blow: one day, Emery will meet the love of her life, and Eva never kisses that boy.

2

Fires Need Lanterns

The bowling alley fire was not the small town's first fire. They have been becoming more and more common in recent years—I wonder, have you had any fires in your own small town?

As she lingered in her bedroom at home, Emery wrestled with wanting to talk to her dads. Something yelled in her teenage brain that she shouldn't go cry on her dad's shoulder, and she was too old for that now. But something much louder screamed through her heart that it was the only way she would ever be ok again. So, she put on her pajamas and walked downstairs, wrapped up in a traditional sarape.

Her pa, Erick, sat on the couch with his feet up on a beige footstool. He was reading a new murder mystery, as he always was at this time of night. He slightly smiled as he read and slowly sipped his tea that he held in his hands tightly, as if he was cold. Emery pulled her sarape tighter around her and sat down on the couch right next to him. He didn't even pause to find a bookmark before closing the pages and setting both the book and tea on the side table so he could pull her into his chest.

And with that, held safe against him, the faucets opened, and Emery burst into tears. He held her even tighter but didn't try to stop her or ask why. She spent about five minutes just crying there in silence. Erick was growing worried, but he just held her tightly, knowing that words would come in time. Sometimes the tears must fall before words are even possible.

Eventually, the tears slowed. Emery moved out of his hold as she gasped, swiping at her cheeks to remove all traces. Erick handed her a tissue as he drew her back in for a hug.

"Are you ready to talk?" he asked as Emery kept inhaling harshly and desperately.

She told Erick everything about her night, right from the beginning and the great debate about what to wear to her first date. What she expected was warm words, hot cocoa, and a speech about boys and toxic behaviors.

What she got was much more bizarre.

Erick cut Emery off from talking and went to the window. He looked back and forth, then drew the curtains closed, before flicking back the corner just enough to see outside.

Emery adjusted herself. She had almost fallen when he got up so quickly. He never acted like this and honestly, it scared Emery.

"Pa? Is everything ok?"

He walked back towards her to kneel in front of her and rubbed her shoulders, "Everything will be ok."

To the already confused young girl, this wasn't exactly

comforting. I, on the other hand, knew that he was both very right and very wrong.

"Tell me more about the fire." He continued.

"Like what?"

"Where did it come from?"

They both heard the back door open, and they jumped. Pa because he had a real reason to be afraid, and Emery because something in her heart knew just as mine did, that everything was changing in this moment.

"Joaquin?" her Pa said, with a shake in his normally steady voice.

"Ya." Erick breathed a satisfying exhale when he recognized the voice.

"Come here, please, babe."

"Sure, just grabbing some coffee."

"It's an emergency." There was a sweetness in his words that didn't quite match the way he looked at Emery. Emery herself wasn't quite sure what made this an emergency. She had heard about traumas at school but didn't think this quite constituted one—she hadn't been hurt, after all—and she worried that instead she would be traumatized by her over-protective parents and their will to never let her really live. She was quickly regretting admitting anything to her pa at all. She worked so hard to get them to allow her to go on a date, and now wondered if this reaction would also mean she would never be allowed to leave the house again.

"What is it, Erick?" Joaquin said as he walked into the room with the coffee pot sill in his hands.

"It's time," Erick responded. He looked at Emery, as if

Emery could not tell that there was something very strange going on. She suddenly felt both her dads' eyes on her and hadn't felt quite this way since she told them once when she was little that she wanted to kiss a boy. Joaquin set the hot coffee pot down onto a pile of papers on the coffee table.

"Fire?" Her dad asked Emery as he walked towards her to take a closer look with his serious deep brown eyes. Erick walked over and picked up the coffee pot, without mentioning that Emery's dad had almost started another fire at that very moment.

Joaquin sat down next to her and gently smoothed Emery's hair off her face. It was a rare moment. Her pa was the more sentimental parent, and her dad rarely gave her sweet moments like this.

"Ya, there was a fire at the bowling alley." She said quietly.

Her dad, Joaquin, had tears in his eyes, and Emery didn't think she had ever seen that in him before.

When someone strong cries, you have to wonder what fate awaits the weak of us.

Joaquin turned and looked at Erick.

"There isn't anything else we can do. I know this isn't what you want, but we have to protect her. I know you know that." Her dad's voice was as strong and steady as ever, but there were tears threatening to spill over and down his face.

Pa looked at the coffee pot in his hands. "Let's have some coffee and make our plan then babe."

Joaquin looked back at Emery. "I need you to go get ready for bed." Erick left and went into the kitchen as Joaquin sat down next to Emery on the couch. Her dad slowly put his hands on her face lovingly, making her look right in his almost black eyes.

"Yes, get ready for bed. We are going to keep you safe; I promise I will never stop trying to keep you safe." Emery looked back at her dad and slowly peeled his hands away from her face.

"Ok." She said and tightened her sarape back around herself and walked upstairs to her room.

She immediately fell face first onto her bed, her feet giving out beneath her. It felt sometimes that the entire universe was plotting against her; she could never quite do anything without having to deal with something new.

Now that she thought about it, she wasn't completely baffled by the behavior of her dads. They never let her do anything besides go to school, and they didn't even want her to do that, it took years of convincing. She remembered staying up all night hearing them argue about whether she could go to school downstairs; it was the only time she ever heard them raising their voice at each other. It only stopped when she crept down the stairs and Erick spotted her listening in.

He ran over and picked her up, lovingly asking why she wasn't in bed. He turned back around to Joaquin and said, "She will be fine going to school. We need my job to keep this home and we need your job to secure our future. This is the choice we are making." Joaquin looked straight at Emery after he said that, not at Erick, and he didn't say another word.

Emery remembered this for years, but never quite understood it. Emery's dad, Joaquin, claimed to be a nanny at a rich person's home. He said that their privacy was crucial, and that's why Emery could never meet them. When she was younger, Emery liked to think her dad was the nanny to a famous pop star. Emery's pa was a financial advisor. Emery did not have any cool theories about who he worked for.

Besides school, Emery wasn't allowed to go to friends' houses, go to the movies, or have any typical kid experiences. This was particularly awful because as we all know, school is all the worst parts of childhood. School is the fights, the bullying, and the crying. What she missed was the late-night giggles, the secrets revealed in a tent, and the kisses at bowling alleys.

The date itself with Levi was Emery's early birthday present. A couple of months before her birthday, she sat her dads down in the living room. They both smiled and held hands. They thought it was such a sweet example of how their daughter was growing older.

"I need to talk to you guys about something very important."

They smiled again and looked at each other.

"I need you to take me seriously!"

Joaquin's face was serious in an instant, but Erick had to cover his joy with his hand as she spoke. He couldn't help but think this new confidence of hers was just about the cutest thing he had ever seen. But Emery didn't want to be cute anymore and it fueled her authoritativeness on this matter even more.

She pulled her laptop out of her backpack and plugged it into the television. The screen filled with a PowerPoint slide of her dads holding her as a toddler for the very first time.

Erick almost lost it, but she gave him a very stern reminder with a look.

"As I'm sure you both remember here, I am as a small child." She pushed the computer mouse, and the next picture was her and her dads last weekend before they had had a barbecue at their friend Dale's cabin like they did every summer.

"Here I am now. I'm sure you can clearly see a difference between these two. So how did we get here you ask?"

The next few slides included all her accomplishments at school and her chores at home. Erick now was crying a bit, though he was smiling still, and Joaquin was back to smirking, not quite sure where it was going. Their giggles turned into stone-cold faces as the slides changed to why she should be able to go out on a date. She regretted using a picture of a grown woman at her wedding immediately and flew past that slide as quickly as possible.

The stone-cold faces turned a little softer around slide 15 when she began to cry a bit about how she worried she would never fall in love. She went back to the first picture they ever took with her and wiped her tears.

"I need you guys to realize, I'm not this little girl anymore." She stood a little taller, drawing her shoulders back in an effort to project confidence. "I am a teenager, almost an adult and all I know of love, all I know of friends, are from movies and books." Here her confident cover slipped, and she looked down, suddenly uncertain. "And it makes me feel like I'm missing out on all the life that makes life worth living." She glanced back up at them, her eyes gleaming with hope. "I'm begging you. I just want one chance. I just want one date. Consider it my birthday present. I won't ask for another birthday present again in my whole life."

Joaquin spoke first, "It was a great presentation."

Erick's smile was large. "Great!"

Joaquin then smiled at Erick as he spoke, "Why don't you head upstairs honey, and we will discuss our decision."

Emery quickly closed her laptop and ran upstairs into her room. She was quite tempted to listen in to their conversation, but she knew if they caught her, her chances would drop like the New Year's ball. So, she sat on her bed and just stared at her wall, waiting anxiously.

Downstairs, her dads had a long conversation that included a few tears, but no fighting this time. They agreed they hadn't really wanted her to miss out on being a teen. They only wanted her to live long enough to be an adult.

They knew it was sad that Emery begged and begged for one date, while all the other kids her age were begging and begging for cars or to stay out all night. Honestly, Erick and Joaquin would have preferred to give Emery the car, but they knew that they had precious few years until she was an adult, and they had to give her a chance.

Erick wanted to keep her safe forever. Joaquin wanted to keep her safe for as long as they possibly could. They both knew that allowing her to go on one date would probably not mean the ending of the safe life they had worked so hard to create for her, unfortunately, it was. But Erick and Joaquin certainly were not happy about the situation, and on the night of the dreaded date, they sat in the backyard drinking beer, being in love, and worrying about Emery.

So no, Emery was not particularly alerted by her parent's strange reaction to the fire and her cheating date, given their past of treating her as if she was the most delicate of fine china. Emery's door slowly opened, and she simply rolled over and slowly sat up as her dads entered her room. Joaquin sat down on her left and Erick on her right, and Emery reached her hands out on both sides with her blanket. They both grabbed the corners so that it now stretched around all three of them, a comforting and unbreakable defense against the dark world outside.

"Sweety, I love you. I always will," Joaquin said, as he leaned in. His dark eyes were still brimming over with tears and Emery searched them for any kind of hint as to why he was so upset when she was, for the most part, fine, albeit with a slightly bruised heart. But she gave up looking for an answer. Maybe she shouldn't have. But I'm only here to tell you what happened, not what should have happened.

"I love you too, dad."

Then Erick spoke. "We both do. I need you to know that everything we have ever done and everything we will ever do is always because we think it's what's best for you." He stood up and put his end of the blanket back around Emery. "Because I love you."

"I love you too."

Erick reached his hand out to her hair and brushed it down. Then he opened his mouth as if he was about to say something but stopped himself.

"I'll meet you downstairs, honey," Joaquin said firmly. Erick nodded but never took his eyes off Emery as he slowly walked out of the bedroom. Then her dad turned around so that they were facing each other. He took her hands into his own and kissed them gently. He pulled slightly at an incoming beard as he spoke.

"Emery, you have to be strong."

Emery couldn't believe it. She finally successfully got her parents to let her go on a date, and now they were more scared than ever. She wondered how many years it would be again before she would be allowed to leave the house.

"I'm fine, really. I didn't even get burned! Plus, I barely liked that guy. Better I found out now what a dick he is right?"

Joaquin tightened his grip around Emery's hands even tighter.

"That's what I am trying to tell you, Emery. You are better than fine. You are great." An awkward pause here allowed for Emery to make things even more uncomfortable with a tight, "Thanks."

But her dad was too far away in thought to hear it.

"But it's not about being great Emery. Almost anyone can be great. It's about being great and brave. That is the unique combination that propels you to success. You have to be brave Emery, the world you once knew is about to crumble beneath you."

This seemed like the type of conversation Emery stood no chance of winning. The last thing she needed after almost dying in a fire, and maybe worse, being stood up for a date, was trying to talk her parents down. She wished deeply that life would just give her one thing at a time.

One fire at a time.

"Ok, look, I'm feeling pretty tired. I think I'll go to sleep. I love you." Emery said as she pulled her soft lavender sheets over her legs. She tucked herself into the sheets and allowed herself to feel safe in them, even if it was only for a moment.

Her dad slowly reached forward. He laid the blanket out over the lavender sheets and kissed her softly on the forehead, "I love you too." Then he slowly backed out of the room. To Emery, who grew up with her parents, it looked creepy and weird. But, to an outsider, well, I thought it was sweet. The door shut, and Emery pulled the sheets in tighter. She no longer trusted anything about this day, not even sleep. And yet it came to her almost immediately.

Not because she was so tired or felt so comfortable in those lavender sheets, but because she was very quickly shot with a silent, and effective tranquilizer.

Two people dressed in all black walked in through the door her dad had walked out of. They opened the window, and two more crawled in from Emery's left side. She wouldn't have seen their faces even if she was awake because they wore masks that covered all but their eyes. Not even her dad saw their faces when he saw them in the hall and ran for his gun— before he too was shot with the tranquilizer.

Her pa watched as Joaquin tumbled to the ground, much as he had the first time they'd met all those years ago at a show. Joaquin had just overheated then, but his friends weren't there, and so Erick had called an ambulance and accompanied him to the hospital. When Joaquin awoke and saw a handsome man by his side, he knew it was all over for him.

This time, as Joaquin hit the ground, Erick was tempted to do the same and to run to his side. But, he knew he had to be smart about this, he stopped himself and, with a deep breath, he slowly crept into the small hiding spot under the floor in the hall closet, the spot they created years ago, but hoped to never use. He had to assume that Joaquin hadn't been killed and that they would just grab Emery and go. That would give him the chance to wake Joaquin and for them to save Emery with the Plan B they had also been planning for years in case this exact thing happened. He knew that he would be more useful not sleeping, and not being discovered at all.

Upstairs, the four people looked down at Emery.

A woman's voice came through one of the masks: "You all check the rest of the house?"

"Clear," one of them responded.

The woman slowly took her mask off and sat down on the bed.

"This is her." The woman put Emery's hand within her own and closely examined both sides. She used her thumb to inspect each part, until she saw a small speck of ash in between her index and middle finger.

"Take her," she said with a blank stare. She walked towards the window in Emery's room and stared out of it, now completely silent.

One of the other mysterious people in all black, pulled down those lavender sheets that Emery had always counted on keeping her safe. He pulled her up into his arms and carried her downstairs, walked over Joaquin's body, past Erick hiding in the floor, and all the way outside to place her carefully and quietly on the floor of a large, all black jeep, next to two other slumbering teenagers.

Emery didn't wake.

As the jeep hurled down the streets, the three teens rolled back and forth across the floor, gaining bruises on every corner that would be the least of their worries soon. Eventually, the jeep arrived at a large silver facility in the middle of the mountains that looked perfectly out of place. The massive silver security gates loomed over a single red booth at the entrance.

Eli was the security guard at that red booth, although no one at Camp Carce really cared or even knew Eli's first name. It sometimes made Eli sadder than he cared to admit. The jeep partly rolled down the window, and Eli's eyes met the drivers. Eli recently grew a long brown beard to try to look more intimidating, even though he already had muscles the size of the jeep's tires. But he couldn't quite get his sweet blue eyes to look as scary as the Keepers, the men and women dressed all in black. The Keeper in the driver's seat leaned a little closer to Eli.

"Fires need lanterns," he said in a rough, but somehow soothing voice.

Eli pulled back his hand that had been on his gun and pushed the bright green button directly next to the bright red button. The gates opened up, and the jeep drove through. The building was large and kept in almost perfect condition. In fact, it looked like a factory that kept the most precious of diamonds, not a prison for the most precious of kids. Black jeeps were lined up like obedient ants in front of the building, and there was one single garage open, out of at least ten garages all lined up.

As the jeep pulled up to the open garage, Emery rolled over. All the Keepers quickly looked back at her body at the same time before sharing a nervous glance. The driver drove quickly into the garage, and they all stayed in the car, with one eye on Emery, until the garage fully closed behind them. As soon as the door closed, they all jumped out of the car and walked away. A moving kid had never happened before, but their job was to get her into the facility, and they never did more or less than their job.

The back door opened, and three more Keepers entered the garage. They opened the back of the jeep and stood there staring at the bodies. These Keepers were also in all black, but they seemed to have a bit more freedom. All three wore tight black t-shirts with black cargo pants and boots. One Keeper was clearly in charge. She had light brown eyes, short black hair, and a tattoo of a massive snake wrapped around her arm. She noticed immediately when Emery moved again, this time with her hand moving underneath her face, like a pillow.

"Her first," she said to the other two, both male. One had wild brown hair that I wished he would fix for the sake of this eerie professional vibe his employment had. The other had gone the opposite route and was completely bald. They pulled Emery's body out of the jeep and started to walk away with her.

"I would like to meet with that one right when she wakes up," the woman with the large snake tattoo said.

The two men carried Emery's body down a brightly lit, almost blindingly so, hallway. They passed large metal doors, akin to bank vaults with large locks on each one and letters in brass above the locks. They reached number 16 and dropped Emery to the ground so they could open the lock and the door. They were not gentle at all, unlike the Keepers who had placed her in the jeep.

The door opened slowly and revealed two small cots, terrible gray walls, and strange drawings covering them. They picked Emery up off the hallway floor, and she made a grunt that made the large men jump a bit. They froze, waiting to confirm that she was still asleep before they brought Emery in and placed her on one of the cots. The bald man stayed behind and looked at her until the wild haired man reminded him, "We have two more to go get."

They left the room (if you can call it that), locked it up, and walked away. Probably thinking at that moment, they would never see Emery again. It wasn't their job to interact with her. They would send friendly Keepers to get her in the morning, and they would continue moving tranquilized teens in and out of jeeps and sometimes planes.

But as the sun came up slowly, Emery woke up before the friendly Keepers came to get her at all, and she woke up to new terrible adventures that were just beginning. She didn't recall going to sleep with a handsome boy lying across from her in a cot. Thoroughly confused, she rubbed at her eyes and slowly sat up. She looked around at the dark and unwelcoming room and did what anyone at any age would undoubtedly do: she called for her dad.

When her dad never came, and the boy didn't stir from her screaming, she decided to do what she did best: think. She pulled out her braids and put it into a bun instead, trying to channel a bit of energy into change. She spoke aloud because the strange, handsome boy was obviously sleeping deeply, and she thought better when she talked.

"Alright, Emery." She rubbed her hands together. "What do we have here? I am in..." She looked around and took a deep breath. "Prison?" She got up and tried to open the massive metal door but failed, so she sat in front of it.

"Well, it's illegal. You can't put kids in prison. Can you? I should have paid more attention in government class. There was the one boy Dave who stole a teacher's purse. Everyone said he went to prison. I wonder if he did, how long would he be in for? Is he out yet? This is not helpful." She looked down. "Ok, I'm still in my pajamas," she said, looking at her blue satin pants and a black tank top. Then slowly she looked up at the boy and adjusted her tank top. She saw him move his cute hand and put it under his slightly curled, almost white-blonde hair.

Then she heard someone walking outside the door. Not completely sure what she was dealing with, she ran back to her cot and pretended to be sleeping. The door sounded like it went through a billion locks and then creaked open. She kept her eyes closed tight in a desperate attempt not to reveal the bad guy just yet, holding onto a childlike hope that the tighter she screwed her eyes shut, the more likely she would be to wake up and this would all be a dream.

Unfortunately, this was not a dream, she would not wake up, and things would only get much, much worse.

3

Camp Carce

Emery laid with her eyes tightly closed and held a flimsy sheet over her head. Some adult who lingered in her told her she should get up and fight, but a child in her told her she would be safest under the sheet. The sounds of six stiff black boots filled the room that had become her new prison. One of the owners of the boots picked Emery up and threw her over his shoulder. It hurt Emery's stomach, but she made a distinct effort not to make a noise. Though her patience was not getting stronger, she slowly opened her eyes as the man continued walking with her on his shoulder and out the door.

What she saw when she opened her eyes was a young woman's light brown eyes staring right back into hers. Emery closed her eyes quickly, feeling as if she had not only been caught, but somehow in locking eyes with this woman; she already allowed these people to win a battle. She took a breath and had to swallow a small piece of her ego down in order to try again. She could feel this ego as it traveled slowly down her throat. Once it was all the way down in the pit of her stomach, she opened her eyes to see what else she could discover about her current situation.

She looked up once more. This time the woman smiled at her. The smile had a strange effect on Emery. She desperately wanted to fight this woman. For a moment she pictured herself lunging at the woman and holding her down with her hand at her throat while asking if her dads were ok. Yet, the woman's villainous smile somehow felt a bit comforting. Sometimes when things are the darkest, the smallest light, even if it's not real, is somehow comforting.

Nonetheless, she closed her eyes again, unsure how to respond. She considered what her first words would be to this strange woman. She was deeply concerned about her dads. But she began to think bringing them up might not be the smartest move. What if her dads were safe? She could be putting them in danger by mentioning them. She began her list at this moment. The list of people she would vow to make sure were ok. It was very difficult for her to focus on this list over the one she really wanted to make; the one filled with names of people she vowed would not be ok.

They entered another silver door, and now Emery couldn't see the woman at all, because she had walked too far ahead. The large man roughly dropped Emery into a dull metal chair in the middle of the room and strapped her in. She did not hold back a noise this time as she fell in like a bag of flour. The straps on the chair wrapped across her chest and up her legs. They were old leather and somehow freezing cold on her usually warm skin. He pulled her down so tight she felt as if she might be forced to die in this chair, and she pictured her dad standing over her telling her to be strong.

Then, separate straps pulled her hands and arms down to

the armchairs and made it impossible to move. She noticed all of the straps were also attached to a large tank to her right filled with water. As if she could do anything but hardly breathe, they tightened her to the chair even more. She wondered if they would electrocute her. It was all she could think of in trying to determine the purpose of the chair.

Emery did not have any interest in being electrocuted, but more than that she now had a list of people in her head to save, that she couldn't stray from no matter what. She started trying to wiggle different parts of her body. Then she began looking around the room at her different options for an escape from whatever strange torture lay in front of her.

The woman that made eye contact with Emery in the hall was sitting in front of her with three large computer monitors. The room walls were uninviting shiny red and looked like they had never had any dirt on them. One wall was filled top to bottom with books. The wall directly behind the woman was filled with vials. One more wall was large black filing cabinets. All meticulously set up by someone who likely found joy in perfection, or was it someone who found pain in imperfection?

The woman with short black hair and piercing eyes, peered around the screens and looked at Emery. She spoke, and that made Emery notice her plump, almost coral lips. She saw the large tattoo of the colorful snake around her arm.

"Amery Esa correct?"

"Emery- Em-er-ee Ah-sa"

This seemed like a strange time for Emery to correct her kidnapper on her name's pronunciation. But Emery decided many years ago never to let someone pronounce her name wrong. Three years ago, when she was twelve, she had her last straw. The substitute teacher began calling her Emery Ass-a. They didn't just say it once, though. She called her by that name all class period. The students, of course, very much enjoyed this easy target that the teacher had set up.

If we are being honest, there is something dark that lives in children. Something tells them to find flaws, to laugh, and to bring others down. Even the brightest and loveliest of adults were mean children, just like everyone else. You probably only remember being nice to everyone, just like the person who hurt you only remembers being nice to everyone.

So, of course, the kids used this material. They called her only Ass-a for about a month with extra emphasis on the ass and sometimes with added drawings or shoves. One night after she had finally cried all her tears, she talked to herself. She spoke to herself in her bedroom as if she was her therapist. She worked through the surface-level issue and knew what she had to do.

No one would call her by the wrong name ever again. She would correct them until they said it right. They would call her Emery annoying-sa after that. They only did it behind her back because she would follow them around, saying her name correctly until they would repeat it.

It was a good and worthy thing to learn. Never let people call you by the wrong name. Although, she arrived to the lesson on a superficial boat. Not wanting to be called an Ass was not the best reasoning for her pride in her name. But sometimes, I suppose, it doesn't matter how you get to the lesson, just that you get there at all.

The woman laughed, "Emery Emery."

"Where am I?" Emery continued with a straight and almost threatening face while being completely helpless otherwise.

"I'm Estrella. Welcome to Camp Carce." She said smiling.

Emery had heard of Camp Carce before. Even a kid as isolated and sheltered as Emery knew about Camp Carce. She knew it as the camp kids never return from. She first heard about it when she was a little girl. The older kids at elementary school would come over to their side of the playground to scare them. Sometimes they would hide in scary outfits under the slide or grab their ankles under the monkey bars. Other times though, they would scare them with stories. Like the legend of BigFoot (who they amended to eat children), the Boogeyman and the camp kids never came back from. It was stories like this that had dug themselves into her mind and nightmares permanently.

More recently, there was a rumor that a boy at her high school went to the camp. It was a boy that Emery knew pretty well. She went to school with him, all growing up. When she was much younger, she had a crush on him, but she doesn't give much value to younger Emery's thoughts. His name was Jake, and he had long brown hair that he would always shake to get out of his eyes.

One day he just didn't come to school. Emery noticed in homeroom only because she was acutely aware of what all people are doing at any given time. After about a week, kids started to make jokes about whether he had died or was sick with the kissing disease. After three weeks, the tone amongst the kids completely changed when discussing Jake. Students called him with no answer, and friends sent a thousand texts and watched as the delivered message never became read.

Jake's good friend Martin had had quite enough, though. He marched up to their homeroom teacher, Mrs. Vell, and explained that this was unlike Jake. He asked her how a student could be missing for a month, and the school could have no information about where he was. There are all types of teachers in this world. There are teachers trying their hardest to make their bosses happy. There are teachers trying their hardest to make the children happy. There are mean teachers and kind teachers. But then there is another blurry archetype of a teacher. There is the teacher who actually cares. Mrs. Vell was one of those. She didn't focus on making others happy as much as she cared about doing the right thing.

So, she heard Martin out and decided to do the right thing. First, she invited him around to the other side of her desk. She looked with him through records to see that Jake had been unenrolled from the school. She then drafted an email that she addressed to the principal of the school. She asked for specifics about Jake's situation and said that she believes students deserved to know what had happened to their friend. Martin was satisfied with her response and the fact that she did anything, so he took a seat and calmed down.

When the students walked into the class the next day, Mrs. Vell sat on her stool facing the classroom. All the students knew that this meant something serious. Usually, Mrs. Vell would greet the students at the door with a warm smile. But when she sat at the stool, it meant she would talk to them about something serious. With all the maturity in them, they quietly and rapidly took a seat because of their respect for Mrs. Vell.

"Good morning. I got some news about Jake." She said, putting her long blonde curls into a bun as she spoke. "He is fine. So, I want to start there." She looked out at the class to make sure everyone was following, and she hadn't lost anyone. "He is at Camp Carce."

She lost one.

Martin stood up and hit his desk. "This is bull shit. You know just as well as we do what people say about Camp Carce."

Emery herself felt conflicted at the moment. She didn't know Jake very well, and he had even made fun of her one time in class. But she did know what people said about Camp Carce. She needed to know more before she decided if Jake was ok or not. She had learned many of the things she once believed as a child weren't real, and at this age, she had become more skeptical than ever. It would have been better had that skepticism been towards the camp and their intentions instead of the kids who told the stories.

"Martin." The teacher said both calmly and sternly, "Please take a seat so I can continue."

Martin took a deep and audible breath to show he was still angry but took a seat.

"I do know." She continued, " I know what you all say about Camp Carce. It's been a legend around here for many years. I remember hearing those things when I was your age as well. That's why I looked into it. I found the Camp website, and I'm happy to show it to anyone here if you want to set up a time. I believe it is a real and safe place. Our principal confirmed to me that they have been in contact with Jake and his family. It was at Jake's request that he didn't want to remain in contact. I think this is a lesson."

She got up from her stool and walked over to Martin, who had shifted from angry to sad. He had his head on his desk, buried into his arm. She gently put her hand on his shoulder while continuing to address the class. " I think it's a couple of lessons. One that we shouldn't make up stories to scare other people."

Emery felt more and more at ease with Mrs. Vell and had shifted from analyzing whether she should intervene to trying to internalize the new lessons. "These stories hurt people." She looked at Martin, "They hurt those we love and those in those situations. Look at how we are feeling because of these stories. Not good. Can you imagine how Jake could have felt when he was going to the camp?" She looked around and walked back to her stool. Martin calmly shifted his head up to listen again.

"Jake probably had these same scary stories in his head. Even though it seems like he is happy there and becoming a better person in a different learning environment. It must have been hard to get the stories out of his head at first. It might be part of why he didn't want to stay in contact with us. He knows how badly our community views the camp." She let her hair back down as she was easing back into teaching and out of sharing bad news.

"The other lesson here is that not everyone stays in your life forever. This will be one of the hardest lessons you will ever learn. But everyone and everything is temporary. Jake chose to move to a new place in his life. We have to respect that and move on ourselves. I know that's not a happy truth, but not all truths are happy. Be as much at peace as you all can with knowing that Jake is safe." Her tone shifted and became a bit less soft. "Any further questions or if you want to talk about anything with me, please put a message in my mailbox." She pointed at the mailbox on her desk that she had painted with daisies, and kids could write her notes.

Emery decided that she would not be writing a note to Mrs. Vell about Jake. She felt like Mrs. Vell had done her research, and she trusted her judgment. She felt that Jake not being at school anymore would not really have any impact on her. That Camp Carce would not affect her. Well, we see now that Emery was quite wrong. Although with the right intentions, we can also see that Mrs. Vell led twenty students down the wrong path. Emery only realized now, at this very moment, that Jake never returned from Camp.

4

Meant for This

Emery underwent an uncomfortable conversation with Estrella in what we will call the testing room. Emery knew a couple of things about survival. Most of these stemmed from her dads reading her stories every night until she got old enough to read them herself.

She knew that she couldn't be too forceful, couldn't fight too hard, because she was strapped to a chair. She was intelligent enough to know that sometimes you have to think before fighting too. The straps on her arms attached to the large mysterious tank reminded her that this was not the moment for her fight. But that didn't mean she wouldn't.

She would fight. She would fight harder than anyone ever had at Camp Carce. But part of her fighting was also keeping her cards close and evaluating the situation entirely before she would launch into attacks. She didn't pick this lesson up only from the stories.

Her dad, Joaquin, taught her this when she was just a little girl. Her dad often talked to her in strange ways like this, as if he was somehow preparing her for battle. He would sit on her bed late at night and tell her stories, always about young girls, always about them fighting their way out of something. Her pa Erick would walk by the room, peek in, but never stayed.

Estrella took some blood from Emery while she was seated and asked her questions about her life. Emery tried to lie only slightly when she answered them. She wanted them to be close enough to the truth that they would believe her lies. But far enough that she wasn't actually helping whatever sinister plot they had in play.

"What's the last thing you remember before being here in this room?" Estrella asked her as one of the Keepers in black outfits inserted a needle into her arm. She had a raspy voice that sounded like it may be lost at any moment.

"I remember just going to bed." This was untrue. She remembered waking up in the room, pretending to be back asleep when the Keepers returned.

"Can you recall what happened last night?"

"I went to bed."

"Can you tell me something about a fire?"

"There was a fire. I don't know. I wasn't very close to it. I think it was at the movie theater. Can I talk to my parents?"

"Eventually, but I need you to work with us before you earn that privilege." Estrella responded with a look of suspicion in her eyes before she continued, "Can you remember any other fires in your life?"

This question sparked a strange reaction in Emery. She started visualizing all the fires she had ever seen. They were vivid, and she felt hot. She smelled the smoke and tasted the flames. Just then, her arms jolted with the thought. Her hands turned a bright red. The men near Emery jumped as they noticed her glowing red hands, and they put silver bags around her hands that felt ice cold. Estrella looked excited and wrote on her pad at high speed.

"That's enough." She said, almost shooing Emery away, who ironically was still strapped down to the chair. The men unstrapped her and one of them threw her over his shoulder as he proceeded to walk towards the door. Emery reached back towards Estrella.

"Wait, wait, I have some important questions." The man carrying her paused for a moment.

Estrella looked her in the eyes, "We have all the time in the world for that."

"Ok great, what the fuck is going on here?"

"We have all the time...later. There are more children, Emery, more things to do. I'm quite busy." She continued writing on her pad then looked up to see Emery still looking at her. "You can take her!" She said loudly, and the Keeper quickly walked out of the room.

Emery tried to internalize more about the building as the Keeper carried her through the halls.

"I can walk." She said while also lightly hitting him on the back. He responded with a grunt and dropped her to the ground. When she got up, he tightly kept his hand on her shoulder. She tried to memorize the empty halls, but more so, she was searching for imperfections, searching for anything that would be a weapon. A crack in the wall or a tile slightly out of the ceiling might be all she needed. Something about her being in this strange, terrible situation felt strangely right.

I knew one thing for sure. Some people like Emery are born to live through terrible things.

The Keepers pushed her back into the room. She got back up quickly. When she looked up, she saw the handsome boy she saw sleeping earlier. His back was to her, but he slowly turned his head, and she saw his deep brown eyes for a moment before he turned back around to the wall. Emery, who always found her joy from others, walked right up and in front of him as the Keepers closed the door. He was wearing blue jeans and a red t-shirt. He played with a string on his pants like it was his first and only job.

"Hi," She said gently, trying to catch his eyes again. He took a deep breath, shook his curly light blonde hair to the side, and looked up at her. "Hi."

That was all our dear Emery needed as a reason to get to know him.

She sat herself down on the cot directly in front of him.

"Camp Carce." She said, looking at their cell-like room. "Who would have thought?" She smiled.

He didn't respond.

"I'm Emery. Who are you?"

He looked up and continued to play with the string but kept eye contact now.

"Philip."

"How long have you been here, Philip?"

"I think it's been about a week." He said while releasing his pant string for a moment to flip part of his ice blonde hair from his face.

"Did you meet that lovely, Estrella lady?"

"No, I have only been taken for regular activities."

"Where are you from?"

"I'm from Colorado."

"Well, hey!" She said, nudging him, "At least we know they aren't stealing kids from everywhere. Maybe we are all locals."

He gave a small smirk that gave Emery just enough energy to continue.

"So, Philip, I have to get back to my parents, and I'm sure you have to get back to other pants with other pant strings to pull at. How should we escape?"

She got up and started looking in every corner of the room for anything she could use or see. Phillip himself was already taken aback by our sometimes odd little Emery. He was trying to think of how to respond. He couldn't actually imagine planning an escape and felt relieved when he was saved by Emery continuing to speak before he had had a chance to respond.

"Why is it so damn cold, Philip?"

"There is nothing in here, Emery. I've looked over and over again. You're wasting your time."

"Wait, go back one minute. What do you mean they take you for regular activities?"

"You should find out soon. Soon we will go through your first daily activity. They will take us to lunch. We go in shifts. At least, I think so. I think because there are so many more rooms than kids that I see at lunch." He said, finally completely pulling a complete string from his pants.

"How do you know lunch will happen soon? There is definitely not a clock in here. Do you have one?"

"No. But it's like my body has adjusted to this new life already. I know when we leave because my body yearns for it every moment, and somehow, I just feel when it's creeping closer." He held onto his stomach and looked up at her almost desperately, and inside he felt incredibly proud of his deep reflections that would surely win over a girl as odd as this.

"Well, maybe this camp isn't so bad, after all. Will we get anything good for lunch?" She asked, mostly wanting to steer the conversation in another direction.

Emery couldn't care less about lunch. She knew that her current situation was quite dire, and inside she felt hopeless and cold, like her environment. She wouldn't show it. She was stubborn in that way. But, before Philip had a chance to answer, she went over to her cot and laid down.

"I think I'll take a nap." She said as she curled into a ball and faced the wall while allowing tears to begin dripping onto the flat and stiff cot. Philip thought his first interaction with his new roommate had not gone well at all. As she slept, he looked at her brown hair that looked so soft he wanted to touch it, and for a moment, just a moment, he felt guilty.

Emery woke to the sound of the large metal door opening. She sat up quickly from her unrestful rest. The Keepers stood at the door, and Emery saw they were new and younger faces.

"Lunch," They said in unison; that wasn't comforting to the ears but instead startling.

Emery got up and straightened her silk pants. She

immediately was embarrassed that more people would see her in her now dirty pajamas, which she knew was the least of her problems, but she couldn't help but feel that it was just as important as the rest.

She pulled all her hair to the side and quickly braided it as she walked out the door. She followed Philip out the door, and the two men followed them closely as Philip led them down to the right where a large metal door, just as shiny as the rest, stood closed and without any handles. Emery wasn't sure how, but they opened. This made her look into the corners to see small black dots that must be cameras surrounding wherever she went. She made a mental note to look for them in her room.

The lunchroom was about half the size of the cafeteria at her high school. There were maybe 20 kids at tables sitting at four different round maroon tables. One table had small children, perhaps in elementary school, laughing as they chatted. One had slightly older kids who looked scared and weren't talking much. The last two had kids about Emery's age whispering to each other. She walked over to the 4th table and sat down. They all stopped and looked at her.

"I'm Emery." She said full volume as Philip sat down next to her.

She was shushed by the youngest-looking girl at the table immediately. She responded in a whisper, "Sorry. I'm new here." They all gave her a dirty look but, most significantly, a guy with skin that matched her own but with reddish-brown almost curly hair. She looked down, and it stung. I've always thought that the problem with kids who have adult problems is that those problems don't replace the torment of being a kid, that still lives in them all the time.

But she knew that she was braver than she ever had acted before, only because she was becoming more and more aware that she didn't have time to waste. But that bravery only disguised her own feelings, her own fears.

Her eyes began to well up a bit. Phillip gently put his hand on her back, and she looked at him. She blinked away any tears as he looked at her and she looked into his brown eyes. She wasn't sure if she was finding comfort in Phillip or release, but neither felt right.

Emery felt saved by women who came shuffling out of a smaller metal door to their right. They were all dressed in black dresses and held large trays filled with what looked like bowls of oatmeal. One of them came to their table and set a tray down.

She carefully put a single bowl down in front of each kid. Emery came last. The woman dropped it off moving slowly, and the others had started quietly eating before Emery had gotten hers. The woman, with her hair, pulled into the tightest bun, placed the bowl in front of Emery. Emery tried to look at the woman for anything she could steal to help her escape. She noticed the woman drop a small piece of paper on the floor. Emery looked at her, and she looked back with silent desperation and then shuffled away, back into a line of other servers all returning to the kitchen.

Emery dropped her spoon and knelt over to pick up the

note at the same time. She quickly tucked it into her pocket and decided to abide by the five-second rule and start using the spoon to eat.

After the women had all left, the kids started whispering one by one while they ate again. Emery wanted to begin plotting their escape but wasn't sure what exactly she was working with yet. She listened to the two kids whispering across the table from her. The young one who shushed her looked like a girl Emery knew once, she had a mean face on, but Emery found that usually, these people are the safest. She whispered with a teen with long hair in a ponytail, whose pronouns she couldn't assume.

"I just miss my brother the most," the girl said.

"I know what you mean, Lor. I think about my mother each night I go to bed. She always came into my room at night and told me all about her day. She knew I would never say anything about mine, so it was like a compromise." They looked down and played with their food a bit before continuing. "I just wish I had told her more about mine."

Emery discovered that the whispers at her table were about memories, family, and the things the kids used to complain about but now missed more than anything.

But while others were floating in their desire to be home with their parents again. Emery was drowning in her plan to make it happen, and more importantly, to save all these other kids. She had already added them to her list of people she needed to save right when she had entered the lunchroom. She decided before her time was up, she needed more information about them. But the problem with her parents not letting her socialize was that she was not very good at socializing. Even I felt uncomfortable each time I watched it. She cut off another kid who was talking.

"Where did you get taken from?"

The young girl across from her shushed her again. The teen she was talking to nudged the young girl after her rude shush and leaned closer to Emery.

"We have to whisper around here. Lor isn't the best about explaining that. It's ok, we've all been there and we've all been where you are. I'm Aiden."

She smiled at their friendly introduction, but the smile quickly disappeared as a terrifying siren went off through the room. The noise bounced off the cafeteria walls, and Emery felt herself get hot as they hit her ears in every direction.

Philip grabbed Emery by the elbow and shuffled her towards the large metal doors of the cafeteria as the siren stopped abruptly. The kids piled in and touched each other as if they were excitedly waiting to enter a rollercoaster. But Emery herself knew that this sort of rushed line was a form of safety. She could tell that hurdling up like livestock had no joy in this context. When she made it to the line, she realized what a missed opportunity this was. She knew there were no exits and no help in the room they were locked into. She knew that no one ever learns anything from not being daring.

She wiggled her arm out of Philip's grasp and moved past other kids to the outside of the crowd. She went to the middle of the cafeteria and climbed onto a table, which shook as if in fear, as she did. She looked at another door on the other side of the cafeteria. Instinctively, she raised her hand to it. It was almost like it was out of habit, but at the same time, it was something she had never done before. As her hand raised, a loud noise popped out from all the vents in the cafeteria.

It was sharp and high and crawled through her body. Her knees shook from it, but she didn't collapse. Suddenly the room was blasting out deep cold water that made Emery fall from the table and hurt her entire right side as her body heavily hit the ground. All the children at the door began to collapse and hold themselves as well. Some of them grasped at each other and coiled into each other like snakes. It had become so cold that the children felt as if they would die at this moment, and many felt grateful for the opportunity. I've seen a lot of pain, but this pain was the worst pain the kids thought the world possibly had to offer. They were soon proved wrong. Suddenly sprinklers with more cold water began raining down onto their freezing bodies with a rigorous force this time, hurling down on them like hail.

This painful shower was the last thing Emery remembered. After this, I watched the water turn off, and the vents close. Some kids who were still moving slowly crawled out the door as it opened. Men in all black, who looked even larger than the other Keepers and had batons on their hips, lined the halls and watched the kids as they moved back to their rooms. These strange men didn't seem affected at all by the children in pain, and I wondered for a moment how in the world a human ever gets to that point. Emery and a few other kids who had passed out from it all were carried by Keepers into their rooms, then again thrown roughly to the floor.

Emery was blue and wet but breathing. Philip, who had

not passed out, looked at her worriedly as I watched him, looking for any darkness just beneath the skin. The Keeper who dropped Emery looked back at Phillip, and the Keeper's eyes said he had words of comfort, but none were delivered. He turned and left the room with a loud bang as he walked out.

Philip wanted to walk over and maybe provide her some warmth. But he could still barely move. So, he curled into the blanket and just hoped that Emery was ok. He laid down and kept his eyes on her to see if she would move. After about 10 minutes, she did. She pulled the blanket over the top of her. The problem with getting warm when wet is that... you can't. So, Philip figured he could take his shirt and pants off and figured as long as he was wrapped up in the blanket, Emery wouldn't know.

Emery woke, though, as he was taking his shirt off, and he felt as creepy as he thought was physically possible. She slowly blinked her eyes, and he pulled the blanket even tighter over himself. She laid down next to him and curled into her blanket, and they stared at each other. Both were lying down, both freezing cold, only one of them terrified.

They stared into each other like somehow that made the whole thing less real. Once they both felt a certain degree of normal again, they drifted off to sleep.

When Emery woke up, she saw that Philip was still sleeping. She decided he was asleep because he made a slight sound like almost a snore, but not quite. She reached into her pocket and was relieved to feel the still a little damp paper that the lady at lunch had handed her before the terrible cold punishment. She checked that Philip was sleeping once again.

Although she had some sort of trust in Philip, she also didn't know Philip at all.

She opened the note and cried silently but with the vigor of an avalanche as she saw her own Dad's handwriting.

Don't make trouble; do what they say. We tried to keep you out of here. If you see me, pretend you don't know me. I love you, honey.

Emery instantly wished she had read this note before deciding to test the system by standing up on that table. She also wished she hadn't tried the system at all because of the terrible pain it had caused all the other children. But sometimes, awful pain comes with great reward. The horrific problem is that occasionally terrible pain comes with zero rewards, and humans just can't seem to tell the difference between the two.

She tried to think about what she gained from the incident. She gained the knowledge that something seemed quite strange. She felt different lately. There was the fire, then the kidnapping, her dad's peculiar note, and that she had so quickly raised her hand toward the door in the cafeteria. She knew that there had been terrible consequences when she did that, but she couldn't really imagine why.

Before she could finish her conclusions, she saw Philip was awake and staring directly at her. He didn't move or get up. He was just looking at her from the exact position he had been sleeping in. At first, she blushed, but then she panicked when she realized he was also looking at the small slip of paper in her hand, which she knew she wasn't supposed to have.

She quickly folded it up and put it into her pocket. She took note that later she would hide it somewhere different because she knew that this note was her most prized possession as of right now, and maybe forever, should she never get to see her parents again.

"It's a note I wrote to myself. It says to stay strong even in the worst of times." She shrugged and played with the corner of the bed. She also wished she had come up with something cleverer.

"Just trying to remind myself how to stay alive." She continued.

Philip sat up in a bit of a hurry. He walked over and sat on the bed next to Emery. It made her uncomfortable. She shifted over to create more space between them. Any attraction she had to him went away when he had moved so close to her so quickly. This would not come as a surprise to Philip.

He knew if there was one girl he needed to get to notice him, it was Emery. He had always been good-looking but never been successful at winning girls over. I think it stems from his first rejection. When Phillip was just a little boy, he finally professed his love for a little girl he liked at recess. He practiced what he would say all night but couldn't remember any of what he had prepared the next day. So, he had this paper out in front of him and read his feelings aloud to her. Before he could finish reading, she was crying with laughter. He ran away and never was quite the same with girls. Now he felt another failure approaching as both Emery and the opportunities to talk and get close to her were ending soon.

"Em, at least we are in this together." He said, starting to nervously play with his pant strings with some lost confidence from her shifting away from him.

What he did not know was that he was already pushing Emery away. She was never one for whirlwind emotions. She always thought it was crazy when people would act as if they loved people they barely knew. In this situation, she felt the same. She hardly knew Phillip, and although she would agree with him because she didn't want to hurt his feelings, she also was thinking we aren't really in this together. She doesn't know him, and her name is not Em.

"I know." She said, trying to see what he was thinking and wondering whether she should trust him. She decided she would probably need his help, and so her best choice was to make him feel as if they were getting close, even though they were, in fact, farther than ever before.

"What do you know about fires, Phillip?"

He looked up, and his piercing brown eyes caught her off guard.

"They asked me about fires too before."

"We have to get out of here, Phillip. What do you know that could help us get out of here?"

"You saw what happened earlier. We can't escape. If you try, you'll keep hurting all of us."

With that, they stopped talking for the evening. Phillip thought that Emery must feel quite hopeless. But that wasn't her style at all. She was planning in that silence.

5

The Smallest Burn

The next morning when Emery woke up, she turned over and saw Phillip doing sit-ups on the floor. He didn't realize she was watching him. She noticed something in his eyes she recognized. It was pain pushed into each sit-up as if each one, each movement, was releasing it. She rubbed her eyes. Then got onto the floor next to him. He paused and looked over at her. She smiled, and his stomach turned. Then they both started doing sit-ups together. They worked out in a stretched-out silence all morning.

The silence finally broke after pushups. Phillip looked over to Emery when he reached his limit. She was still going. Emery used to do pushups every night before bed, and she thought nothing of it. But Phillip, well, this was his worst nightmare. His arms started shaking, and his elbows gave out. He had to beat her. His eyes filled, and he let out a few tears as he fell to the ground.

He got up, wiped his face, walked over to the bed, and kicked it, which made such a loud echo throughout the room that Emery fell to the ground and looked up. Phillip stood with his hands in fists and shaking, looking at a wall. Emery wasn't used to this behavior. She would be the first to admit she wasn't only protected by her dad's. They sheltered her. But shelter is such a fascinating word. It's supposed to be a good thing. We need shelter. We crave shelter. So how come sometimes it can strangle us?

She got up and put her hand on Phillips' back. He pushed it away.

"Just give me a fuckin minute."

She went and laid in her bed and began overthinking the male psyche. A couple of moments later, he came and sat on her bed.

"Sorry. I was just taught that men should be strong."

Emery rolled over and looked up at him.

"Who taught you that?"

He had to be very careful here. He should have changed the conversation topic and learned more about Emery and her plans, powers, and weaknesses. But when he looked into Emery's eyes, it was like he had no control over what he was saying at all. "Everyone. I lost playing soccer to a girl, and the consequence was a good punch to my nose at home. Then when I went to school the next day, a punch to the nuts from my friends. I try not to lose anymore, especially to a girl."

"Don't you think that's letting the bad guys win? You're no less of a man for those things, and you're no less of a man for doing anything."

In the air hung consideration, but it was quickly cut. "Are you still thinking of escaping?"

"How many kids do you think are here?" Emery asked.

"I think the question you should be asking is how many Keepers are there."

"The men and women in all black?"

"Yep."

A knock on the door.

The door opened, and a Keeper stood there. "Emery bathrooms."

She got up and felt relieved to have some time away from Phillip. She hadn't even kissed a boy, and here she was, living with one. She didn't really know how to be or act, and she couldn't help but be attracted to Phillip, disgusted by him, and neither all at the same time. She wondered if it was this complicated with every boy. You and I both know that it is.

The Keeper led her to one of the large metal doors, and when she opened it, Emery found a massive locker room. A girl with short blonde hair and sharp features greeted her at the door.

"Hey, I'm Maya." She said with what sounded and looked like forced kindness. "Follow me and keep up."

Emery looked back at the door closing and the disappearing Keeper and wished she could stay with them, knowing she preferred a large ominous villain to a rude teenage girl.

She followed Maya down a hall of lockers towards a wall of washers and dryers.

"Throw your clothes in one of these. Don't fully wash them. You don't have time. Your Keeper will return in 1 hour. So, if you put your clothes in the washer for 20 minutes, then take them out and put them in the dryer for 30, you'll have clean clothes. You also have one set of clothes to change into from the camp." she said, handing Emery a neatly folded white shirt and white pants.

Emery awkwardly stripped naked and put her old and new clothes into the washer. She had never been naked around anyone of any gender. She only had two hands to cover with, so she chose one arm across her boobs and her other hand covering her vagina. To make matters worse, Maya laughed at her. Then she opened one of the nearest lockers and threw a sizable brown towel at Emery. I think it's important to note that this towel was initially white and that we should all be immensely grateful for clean towels when we have them. Emery quickly wrapped herself in it and started the washer.

Maya took Emery next to a row of showers with brick walls between each.

"Ok, here are the showers. Obviously, choose one. Take a shower, take a shit, get ready to leave." She looked at a watch on her wrist. "You have 50 minutes left." She walked away as she said this and sat on a nearby bench with two other girls, all wrapped in towels. Emery looked for a free shower, but the hair on her arms stood up as she heard the three girls chat and giggle.

She got into the shower carefully. This was quite heavenly, and it was the first time she had been alone since arriving. The water started and was lukewarm at best, but she couldn't imagine anything more pleasing as it ran down her body. She squirted some of the soap from the canister attached to the wall.

She liked to connect objects with power. So, she looked

down at the white swirled soap in her hands. She decided this soap was going to wash away any lingering fear. This soap, she told herself, when it touched her body, would give her the strength and bravery her dads always told her she had. She smiled at the thought.

She covered herself in the soap and watched as it washed off her body. Imagining the dirt and sweat was all the negative things she didn't need anymore. She pointed her head straight into the stream of the water and cried a couple of happy tears. Something as simple as a shower can be taken advantage of, but she cherished this moment. In fact, she cherished it so much that every shower following for the rest of her life was somehow more luxurious than it ever deserved to be.

When Emery got out of the shower, she was relieved to see the three girls had gone. She wasn't quite sure what to do next, and she went and switched her clothes from a washer to a dryer. She sat down on one of the benches and was surprised when a younger girl came and sat down right next to her. She had red curly hair and freckles covering her body that Emery was already quite jealous of.

"Hi, I'm Rose."

"Emery." She said, reaching her hand out.

"What are you in for?" Rose said smiling

Emery laughed, "I'm beginning to think it's related to a fire. You?"

"Same, I lit my school on fire."

Emery's eyes widened, "I'm sorry, what?"

Rose punched her in the arm a bit, "Oh, don't be scared. It wasn't on purpose, and literally, no one was in it. It was late at night. My friends and I had just tee peed the place. My friends all ran away when they saw cop car lights. I didn't see them. But when I turned around, and I was alone in front of our tee peed school with cops right there. I panicked. Lit the whole place up by accident. I ran and ran. Just when I thought I had gotten away. Smack." She said, clapping her hands. "Ran right into a Keeper. I was sleeping within seconds."

Emery accidentally chuckled, "Sorry, I know it's not funny. It's just..."

"Kinda funny? I know. What did you light up?"

Emery paused; she had not considered yet that she was the cause of the fire. But pretended in the moment that she knew exactly what this girl was talking about. Her end goal was to lead them each to safety, and she knew trust always comes before leading anyone anywhere.

"A bowling alley, I think. I saw the guy I was supposed to be out on a date with there, and he was kissing a girl I hate."

"Yikes, that's a deep burn."

"It's a burn for sure. But not too deep. It felt like it at the moment, sure. But once you get kidnapped and trapped in a weird-ass facility, it has me starting to think that burns go a lot deeper than that."

Rose smiled, "I like you, Emery."

"I like you too, Rose" She leaned into her as Rose got up, and she whispered, "and I'm going to get you out of here."

Rose chuckled at the thought, then went to a dryer, pulled out her clothes, and gave Emery a nod after she dressed and left the room with a Keeper who was on the other side of the door when they opened it.

Emery spent the rest of her time watching the dryers spin and thinking about boys. She wondered if she liked Phillip or if she was just literally trapped in a room with a handsome boy, and there was nothing more than that. Her relationship with boys was quite complicated at this time, well honestly, it was pretty non-existent. She knew she was attracted to boys and not girls. She felt something in her she couldn't quite explain when she saw a cute boy. But so far, she didn't really like any boy. There were boys at her school who were mean, and the only one she ever liked betrayed her.

There was Phillip, who seemed quite mean himself, which made her wonder if a good one existed. She wondered whether she would be alone forever. What's so funny about life is that we all have this thought at some point, and still, eventually, we all get shattered by love.

The buzz went off, and she put on her clothes and left the room to find the Keeper. She had an idea this time, though, and as they walked, she spoke.

"So, what is this place for real?"

The Keeper looked down at her and then away. He didn't look angry, though. It was almost as if he hadn't heard her at all, and instead just a squeak from her direction. Emery kept talking, but the Keeper didn't respond at all and didn't even show any emotions as she tried to budge him. He just opened her door, and she walked in. She was quickly aware of Phillip sitting in his bed, playing with his pant strings again.

She walked over and sat at the edge of her bed.

"Does that cool down thing work everywhere? Like even in the locker rooms?"

"Ya, even in here. " He said, pointing to the corner where there was a hole in the wall. She hadn't noticed it before, and she jumped on the bed to get closer. Inside the hole, she could see some sort of valve that must pop out and cool down the entire room. She sighed and walked back over to her bed. She started knotting up her sheet to see if it could be thick enough to cover a hole like that.

"What are you doing now, Em?"

"Wondering how many sheets we would need to plug all the holes in this place."

"It's too powerful. It would just shoot it right out."

She dropped the sheet, frustrated. Phillip came over and sat by her, and he put his hand over her hand, and she pulled it away. "Sorry, I'm just not comfortable being touched."

"Ok, whatever, I was just. No. Whatever." Phillip said, angry again as he got up and returned to his cot. A loud knock broke the silence that followed at the door, and they both jumped up, looking at each other.

"What now?" She whispered to Phillip.

"I have no idea. It's not a usual time for them to be by." He said with eyes so wide they looked as if they would never shut. The door slowly opened but they couldn't see a Keeper. They just heard a deep voice.

"Emery"

Emery got up and walked out, relieved for another break from Phillip, who she was learning seemed to believe he just deserved her affection for merely being alive.

Phillip knew he was not winning her over. There were moments where they felt together. But he also knew it wasn't enough. He had gotten this job because of his looks, age and because he had been living alone on the streets when they found him. When they told him he would be going under-cover, he had to win over this strange girl he wanted to prove that they hadn't gotten the wrong boy. But he didn't see any other paths, any way out, any way that he had been the right boy for the job. He pictured the ice-cold rain Camp Carce poured on small children and wondered what they would do to him when he failed.

6

Scars Always Hold Secrets

Emery was both extremely confused and extremely relieved to quickly realize that the Keeper who came to get her from her room was none other than her dad, Joaquin. In fact, in coming to this realization, a part of her who was just a small child wanted to cry and scream in his arms. But she held on. She let the tears stay battling to come up in her chest, and the screams remained taunting her in her mind instead.

He was dressed all in black as one of the Keepers. When she walked out the door to her room, he winked at her, and it made her feel like her insides melted. All she wanted to do was hug him, to fall into his arms, and have her bring her home. But he didn't. He kept his back to her and walked with her down the halls. She let a tear slip as she followed him. She was so close to him and yet still so far away.

He opened another identical steel door and let her walk in first. It was a small room with nothing more than a small metal desk in it. He closed the door behind her, and to Joaquin's own surprise, he started crying when Emery slammed into his arms with vigor. He cried into her hair as he held her so tight, they both wondered whether he would ever be able to let go again.

Her pa, Erick, cried quite often. He always told her that crying was natural and healthy, and she should cry whenever she had a chance. But her dad didn't seem to agree. She remembered so vividly when he lost his job of 20 years at the grocery store pa cried, and Joaquin stared into space stone cold. She remembered when he lost his mother. He bit his cheeks to keep the tears back until they bled. But here he cried, and it brought Emery the comfort she needed, the reassurance that everything really was fucking terrible right now.

He pushed her away and wiped his tears with his sleeve.

"We don't have much time, honey."

"What's going on?"

"We knew they might take you one day. That's why we sheltered you for so long. That's why I spent so many years trying to get a job here. Your pa and I spied and spied until we linked up with a few of the cafeteria workers. After going on a couple of dates with one, we were able to get me a job in the cafeteria. But these people know I am not a Keeper and have no business being with you, so we have to be quick." He pulled her in and wiped a tear from my cheek. "You're here because you're different, Emery."

They heard the sound of one of the large metal doors closing nearby, and he continued after a small identical jump from both of them.

"You have power. You have the power to start fires."

She didn't know how to take this in. But she also didn't

know how to understand anything that had happened to her recently, so she felt she could digest more news that made no sense.

Sometimes we can be completely lost in life, but we have no choice but to keep moving around in the absolute dark.

"I'm going to get you out of here. Eventually, they will kill you if you stay. They are using you flamethrowers in order to find ways to stop your power, and they use the kids up until they kill them."

He put his rough hands on her shoulders.

"I have a plan. You can escape with your power, but we have to turn off their cold water systems. I will turn it off tomorrow after lunch but while you're still in the cafeteria. You have to just trust that it's off because I have no way to tell you. We are in the north mountains, not far from Dale's cabin if you head the right direction. Then I need you to remember the stories I told you. You have to trust that you have the power and that you can use it. I've heard them talking about you. You're more powerful, and they are trying to determine why."

"I don't understand. Won't you get in trouble? What would I even do?"

Another door closed nearby.

He pulled her in tight, "There isn't time, Emery. Your pa and I love you so much. Tomorrow after eating, but before you're dismissed." He kissed her on the forehead, and she wished she had been able to capture the kiss like a rare butterfly, but it escaped, as they always do.

"Use the fire to destroy everything. Without the cold, they have little defenses. We have to go." Another tear fell from his eye as he pushed her out the door. A crew of Keepers was coming out a door to the right, and he picked up a jog to get her around the corner. They walked quickly back to her room without looking back. He opened the door, quickly closed it, and left. It felt like a dream. It had been so fast and had given her everything and taken everything away at the same time.

Phillip was sitting back on his bed again.

"What was that all about?" He asked.

Emery wasn't quite sure if she should tell Phillip what happened. When her dad told her she would escape, she immediately assumed she would actually be releasing all the children. She didn't know if telling Phillip would make it easier for her, and she decided to keep it to herself until she had thought about this a bit more.

"Just more questions about my life before this."

The door opened again, and Emery chuckled a bit. She felt more active and popular in this prison than when she had been at home. But, this time, it wasn't her dad. It was two large Keepers she hadn't seen before with horrifyingly deep voices. "Phillip!" They shouted into the room. Phillip looked at Emery with worried eyes, then got up and left with the men.

Emery took this time to take out her father's note and read it repeatedly until she felt at home again. She felt comforted and like everything would be ok, all she needed was that moment with someone she loved. She read it and read it until she fell asleep into the comfort and peacefulness of her dad's simple words.

Phillip was not having as peaceful of a moment. The two

men took him to the testing room, the room that Emery had gone to when she first arrived at the camp. Estrella sat with her legs crossed in front of the chair as the men roughly pushed Phillip into the cold seat in the middle of the room.

"Phillip." She said, taking a deep breath. "Should we have taken you in?"

"Of course!" He said like he was a small child again. "I've only had two days with her. I just need more time to find out more."

"And yet in two days, she has been quite the problem." She pulls a clipboard from the desk.

"Let's take a look here." She now traced her colorful dragon tattoo on her arm as she set the clipboard back down. "It looks like she received a mysterious note, she tried to use her power, and more recently, she got an unauthorized visit from someone."

Phillip knew he was in trouble now. He wasn't surprised. His whole life, he had tried to do what he was told. He tried to be the person all these adults wanted him to be, but he was never good enough. He wasn't good enough for his own parents when they told him to sell drugs on the street. He wasn't good enough for the judge when he decided to send him to juvi. He wasn't good enough in juvi when he studied and studied for school and still failed. He wasn't good enough for the girl he met in the streets that he had fallen in love with, but she had returned to her family and never found him again. Now he wasn't good enough for Estrella all because he wasn't good enough for Emery.

"Something is going on, and you need to find out what,

or you are off the job." She smirked and continued tracing her tattoo.

"If you are off the job, I'm not sure that you have a place here. I'm not sure that you need to be here at all. You don't have powers. Turns out you aren't very charismatic. But also, you know far too much. You spent two weeks roaming these halls before Emery arrived." She shook her head like the many people who had shaken their heads at him before.

"You are in a tight spot." She stood up and got so close to him he could smell the old coffee on her breath. "And now it's much tighter." She closed her hand into a fist as if she was crushing something.

"I understand." He said, completely understanding that they would kill him if anything else happened with Emery and also understanding that something else would definitely happen with Emery.

"Ok, you can go."

He stood up and walked out the door. The Keepers followed him down the hall only so that Emery could see them when they dropped him off and not get suspicious.

Phillip spent the rest of the evening really considering his options. Emery spent the rest of the evening with her back turned to Philip, discovering something that would forever change her life. She curled up and pointed just her finger up. When she thought about it, a spark would burst from her finger. She only did it a couple of times. Within the smallest moment, she accidentally started a small fire on her blanket.

But the smallest of fires can become the mightiest.

She quickly put it out and then reflected on how she got

here, how she didn't know that she had had this power. No one did, besides her dads and me, of course. She had never tried to set anything on fire before, and yet here she was, relying on some deep-down power that had only just been revealed to her.

You're probably wondering how her dads and I knew before Emery. When Emery was a young girl, and before her dads adopted her, she was in a fire at her foster home. She only remembers parts of this story. But I remember every moment. Emery was only five at the time, and all she knew was the constant shuffling from one foster home to another. She had been at this new foster home for only a few months and was absolutely hating it.

The mom and dad were actually kind of nice, which was a drastic shift from the last home. In her previous home, she remembers getting hurt a lot, but had a really difficult time remembering exactly how she was being hurt. But regardless, she was happy that she wasn't getting hurt as much at this new home. Although the mom and dad were nice to her, her foster sister Daisy was not so nice.

She was probably a teenager, but she looked like a full adult to Emery. She had short blonde and straight hair and would be pretty if she hadn't been so very mean. Emery watched the girl tease and even sometimes hit these two brothers who were tied at the hip and always let Emery play with them. Emery was too young to understand what was happening. Since most of her experience had also involved violence until this point, she believed that that was quite normal and how everyone lived, so she thought little of it. It wasn't until her dads became her parents that she slowly learned how people should actually treat each other.

One cold and dark Monday, everything changed in that foster home. Daisy was on her way to taunt the brothers, who were trying to teach Emery to play an old game that she was too young to understand, jacks. The boys would bounce a ball and try to pick up as many jacks as they could. Daisy walked into the room and hit the older boy in the head with one of the largest books in the house. This made the younger boy, who was probably about 10, enraged. He stood up from the game and found his voice.

"Stop that right now, Daisy! Just go away!"

"Wooow," she responded, circling the boy as if she was a devious shark. "Look who got some guts. How about I take those guts out and feed them to your older brother?" She said, shoving the boy to the ground.

The older brother's eyes shifted. He was only a year or two younger than Daisy and never seemed to be bothered by her. But, for some reason, this moment was different. He stood up quickly.

"Both the boys are on it today!" She said, cackling.

Her cackling was cut short quickly by the flames that had suddenly engulfed her body and were jumping to other parts of the house like the bouncy ball they had just been playing with. The older brother grabbed his brother and ran out of the house. Daisy dropped to the ground and rolled in circles, trying to get the fire out on her clothes. But by the time she had put the fire on her clothes out, the fire around her had grown too large for her to escape.

Small and fragile Emery sat there with a couple of jacks in her hand, mesmerized by the terror. She watched the fire grow. No one taught her what to do in a fire. She also didn't like seeing Daisy scream in pain. She jumped at one of the screams and reached out to try to help Daisy. When she did, the fire reached up and bit Emery's elbow.

Before she could reach in again, she felt a large firefighter in fire gear pick her up and carry her out of the house. She looked back around her arm and watched Daisy burn through teary but confused little eyes. When she got outside and the woman handed her to her foster mom, she just kept pointing at the house and saying, "Daisy's still there."

But they never brought Daisy back out of the house. In fact, Emery was the last thing that they brought from the house at all. The rest they watched burn to the ground.

Her dads knew about this incident only because the agency explained the burn scar on Emery's arm.

Now that Emery laid in bed planning an escape that she really had no control over, she thought about this. She looked at the scar on her elbow and put her finger across it. She wondered if she had been the one who killed Daisy. These were her last drifting thoughts as she fell asleep. Tears dripped from her eyes until a dream of being back home and doing homework in her lavender bed sheets had replaced the pain.

She woke up in the morning to Phillip doing some push ups in the middle of the room. She watched him for a bit before he noticed and stopped.

"How'd you sleep?" He asked in a kinder voice than the one he had been using so far.

"I slept ok. What about you?"

"Ok, I guess too. You know, all things considered." He said, shrugging. Today felt a bit different already. Her interactions with Phillip before this had felt kind of forced on her. She only liked him because she was stuck with him, but something about him had felt ungenuine. Today though, something in his voice felt very real.

When the Keepers came to get them to give them restroom time, she watched every door and every face for signs of her dad. She wanted to see him one last time before she tried to escape this afternoon. She wanted to speak to him, to be reassured that it was real. To be reassured that she wouldn't harm anyone in her attempt at escape. But there was no sign, no reassurance. She would have to walk blind and hope that sight would follow.

Lunch came closer and closer, and Emery felt a bit more anxious with each breath she took. In the afternoon, the large steel door opened, and two Keepers stood there. Emery and Phillip looked at each other and stood up for the lunch that would change everything. But when they walked towards the door, the Keeper put his hand out to Phillip. He spoke, which was more than Emery had thought Keepers were capable of.

"Only the girl. Estrella wants to see her."

"What about lunch?" Phillip asked.

"You'll go to lunch soon. Keepers will be by for you."

Emery took a deep breath and left with the Keepers. They walked her to the testing room, and her thoughts came in a storm.

Did they capture her dad? Would the plan be broken? Why

did Estrella need to see her? Why now? Would her dad cut the cold, and she wouldn't be there to do anything? Should she run now? Should she escape now? What was the safest choice for the children? Will they just kill her now, and that would be the end? But before she could answer any questions or form any helpful thoughts, she was back in a medical chair staring at Estrella.

"Hello Emery, how is your stay so far?" She smirked.

Emery didn't respond.

"Ok," she said, rolling her eyes as if Emery had no reason to be in a sour mood.

"Look, girl. You might as well get used to me. We are going to spend a lot of time together." Estrella said, looking Emery deep in her eyes.

Emery didn't respond and looked at the ground quickly, not wanting to show strength, weakness, or the tears she had crawling up her body.

"We want to run some more tests today." Estrella continued, now averting her own eyes back to a clipboard in her lap.

Emery tried not to let her chest puff as she sighed in relief. She thought quickly about whether she should ask about lunch. She was curious, but she didn't want to make Estrella suspicious either. Just then, she continued, tracing the colorful snake lightly on her arm.

"You will make it for lunch because this afternoon I want to keep it short. I have some specific tests in mind. Then later expect some more extensive time with me here."

She got up and pulled her into a door on the other side of the room. Unlike the repetitive silver metal doors, this one was a shiny red door. Her arm held Emery's so tight it would eventually bruise as she pushed her into the new room. It was an entire steel room with one window looking into it. Emery looked around for an escape as always, but this room was even worse than the others and was void of anything but the metal walls and a single window. Within this same moment Emery noticed Estrella was looking at her through that window. Emery felt like an animal in a cage, and suddenly understood the sadness in their eyes she always noticed since she was a child. Suddenly Estrella's voice, sounding rougher than usual, carried into the room on some sort of speaker that Emery couldn't locate.

"I brought you to this camp because you have something that needs to be fixed. There is a problem with your body that we will help you with, in fact I believe we are very close. You were brought to us by luck Emery, despite what you feel."

"Stop calling it a camp," Emery said, unable to hold her tongue.

"Can you start fires?"

"No," Emery said, staring straight at Estrella.

"I need you to start a fire."

"I need you to release the other children and myself." Emery responded, feeling tougher now that there was a window between them, ignoring the clear understanding that the window was not making her safer at all.

Estrella took down some notes.

"Interesting. Why would you be so worried about these children you don't even know?"

"Release them and I'll stay."

Estrella laughed and continued, "We won't be answering to your orders, Emery." She smiled and pulled up her hair into a bun.

"Although, this does give me a couple more options. Hear me out Emery." Estrella looked around her own room to make sure no one else was there.

"If I agreed to release one child, would you agree to make a fire for me?"

"Yes." Emery said almost before Estrella finished speaking.

She picked up a walkie-talkie and spoke through it.

"Yes, bring me the Allen girl."

"Emery, if I bring you this child and you don't start me a fire. You're sealing her fate, not your own. She will not stay here at camp, and she will not return home for violating camp rules. Trust me, we take camp rules very seriously."

"You'll kill her."

Estrella smirked and took some more notes, then looked back up to Emery.

"Just start the fire. You've gotten all you can from me and I think you are completely aware of that. Keep pushing it and this deal will become your nightmare. You've revealed too much about what you want already."

A moment later, a Keeper handed Estrella a young girl who looked maybe five years old with her brown hair in pigtails. Estrella held her tightly by the shoulders, so tightly even I wanted to intervene. She looked straight at Emery and nodded.

Emery decided this was actually a win-win situation. She would get to practice more for her escape, and she would possibly be able to save this little girl. She also didn't want to try her hardest, though. She wasn't quite sure how all of this worked, and she felt the need to save up her power for the upcoming escape, which was all she could keep thinking of.

She held her hands up. She pictured herself playing with the small flames in bed when a small flame came slowly lifting from the palm of her hand. She looked at Estrella, who looked delighted, but when she noticed Emery looking at her satisfied, she shook her head no and grabbed one of the little girl's pigtails in her hand.

Emery felt hot as Estrella put her hands on the girl. Emery's anger flooded like fire through her veins as she looked down at her hands again. She wanted to feel flame in her hands, and in a flash, balls of flame appeared hovering only slightly above her hand. Emery was so mesmerized she stared down at them, forgetting every detail of her current situation. The fire felt like pieces of herself lifted into the air with each orange and red flame. Estrella pushed the young girl back to the Keeper and started writing vigorously. Her voice suddenly broke Emery's trance in the room.

"Great," Estrella said, "I have a lot of work to do, Emery, before I see you this evening. But this is important. I want you to remember this feeling. I want you to remember these flames in your hands, the anger in your body." She paused. "And I also want you to remember the cold. The terrible showers you caused yesterday, the little girl you put at risk today, and that any more rebellions with your new power will be punished with lives."

Emery dropped the flames and watched them go out at

her feet. She looked at her hands and noticed a slight red glow remaining for just a moment. Estrella left the window. The moment that Emery saw Estrella leave the window, she turned and threw her hands out as if they had been harboring a secret and watched a massive partially blue flame burst across the room just as Estrella opened the other door. Emery walked out as nothing had happened, although Estrella stuck her head back in the room, feeling the remaining heat even though the room had extinguished it quickly.

She looked at Emery and pushed her to the two Keepers that stood near her. They grabbed Emery by both her arms to lead her back to her room, as her hands glowed red down the hallway.

7

The Start of
Something New

When Emery returned to the room, her red hands had finally become flesh color again, and she contemplated what she would tell Phillip about what happened. But to her surprise, Phillip didn't even bother to ask her what happened. Instead, he laid in silence, staring at the ceiling.

This made her consider her future if she was unsuccessful at escaping. Would she one day be more like Phillip? Would she too become hopeless and desperate?

Then remembered she already was.

But I can tell you that while she may have been desperate, a spark of hope was waiting nearby.

Emery and Phillip spent the next hour asking each other the most random questions they could think of, a game that Emery used to play with her dads on long car trips to pass the time.

"If you could have any job in the circus, what would you want to have?" Emery asked as they laid on the ground, heads near each other and bodies in opposite directions.

"I think I would want to be the lion keeper. I just want

to feel in charge of something so large. I saw a lion at a zoo once, and all I could think about was what it would feel like to be so strong, to be king of something. No one would ever mess with me. Me and my lion." Phillip responded, turning his head and looking at Emery. "You?"

"I would be a trapeze artist. I saw them once at a circus in my town. They looked so free flying through the air. Honestly, it just looked really fun. I just want to live my life having fun, not always putting on a dangerous show, you know?"

"I guess," Phillip said as if he hadn't really been even listening. Possibly, because he wasn't listening, he was trying to think of a clever question that could possibly impress her.

"Ok, I got one, Em. What do you think was the first time that you ever,"

The Keepers opened the door, and Emery and Phillip jumped up. Phillip felt like he had to remember his brilliant question for later, if he had a later with her, of course. Emery, on the other hand, felt anxiety rush through her fiery veins. Emery was about to branch out and do what it took to free herself and others. She was born with this bravery but had never been called on to use it. So, although she felt the courage rooting her, she also felt fear sprouting from those branches.

They walked silently through the halls. Phillip reached his hand out and grabbed Emery's, and Emery let him. The Keepers opened the door to the cafeteria, and Phillip and Emery entered. Phillip whispered something to her, but she couldn't quite hear it. Even though he was right next to her, suddenly everything felt distant and not quite here at all. They sat down at one of the tables with the other teenagers. The boy with reddish brown hair and deep brown eyes, asked Phillip about his journey here. Emery watched the door out of her peripheral and tried to look interested in the conversations.

This was not a well-thought-out plan. She would try her hardest. But now she realized she was facing multiple issues. She wasn't sure when her dad would turn the cold off. She wasn't sure how to open those doors, as she couldn't likely force them open with fire. When the first round of kids had their lunch delivered, she took note of anything she could catch on fire, on each of their trays, even suddenly noticing what layers of clothes she would be willing to burn without guys like Phillip seeing her entire body.

The doors opened again, and more ladies walked out with trays of food that they delivered to Emery's table. She waited for each of the cafeteria women to leave, and then she made her move. She leaned into the center of the table and, in a loud whisper, got everyone at the table's attention.

"Listen!" she said in a hushed yell.

They all listened because Emery both scared and intrigued them. But the boy with the dark eyes made her pause for a moment before continuing.

"We are getting out. The cold is going to be turned off. I'm going to need your help. We will get out through those doors. I doubt my fire is enough to open them. But maybe all of ours is. I'm also throwing everything flammable in it at that door."

Everyone looked at each other, and their eyes all spoke differently. Macy, a rude girl with striking gray hair, had eyes screaming fear. Another teen's said hope, another laughter, and another fear. But the eyes doing the most work were none other than Phillip's.

"Eat first." Emery continued, "Eat quickly. I know you guys think I'm crazy, or maybe you think nothing of me at all because we don't know each other. But none of that matters. It's not about us. Look at how many other little kids there are here. We have one chance. We can't miss a chance. You don't want to be trapped in this place till they kill you without having ever put up a fight, do you?"

None of the teens responded to her, besides with cold, frozen looks. Her confidence melted a bit in her skin. "I need you guys, and I have no other choice." She picked up her spoon and put it in the oatmeal, putting her head down so they would see the tears forming in her eyes. "As soon as I'm done eating."

There was no more whispering from the teen table after that. They all just watched Emery as she ate her oatmeal quickly while looking around at everyone but them. None of them really believed what she had said. But none of them thought they had much more to lose, and it would be just as much a surprise to them what they would do when she stopped eating as it would be to you.

Emery took in her last bite of oatmeal and now looked at her fellow teens one last time. Then she stood on the table like she did the day before, but this time only Phillip noticed her knees shaking as she did it.

Emery waited a moment, with her hands at her sides like lit dynamite, to see if the cold would start. Everyone's eyes shifted from her to the vents, preparing for the pain of the ice-cold rain. When no cold was released from the vents and hundreds of eyes stared at her, she lit her hands-on fire and threw a massive ball of fire at the door. It was larger than the one she had shown Estrella, but her hands craved more. She looked down at the teens, who, to her disappointment, had not even stood up. She looked to the door, which didn't have Keepers running in yet.

"Throw your plates, food, extra clothes, anything to the ground!"

The tables with the younger kids acted first and threw them all to the ground, with screams of children going to war. Then those tables started running and lighting small balls of fire towards the door. At this point, the teenagers got up and began to point their hands at the door, and now they had a wall of flames appearing in front of them. The heat from the flames and the fear was now crowding the air.

It had all happened so fast and yet so slow. Phillip stood up when the teens did. But he was not feeling as triumphant as the others. He knew that door would not open. He knew that these doors were fireproof and that the force and heat would have to be unthinkable to open them. But he also knew that one of the buttons to open the door was just in the kitchen, not far from the door.

He wasn't sure why. If he could look back on it now, he might still say because he had grown afraid of his boss, Estrella. But, from watching it myself, I'm inclined to think that Emery sparked something in him. Did he like her? I don't know, but I know she changed him. I suppose, in the end, it doesn't really matter if you like someone as long as they changed you, then time was never wasted.

Phillip walked towards the kitchen. All the kids played with their fire and targeted the doors, and no one noticed him walk behind them in all the commotion. He opened the kitchen door and saw the staff had all left, likely ran away knowing they had no real way to fight the children. The Keepers, at the same time, opened the steel door on the other end and began running in. The middle school children screamed as they grabbed one of the kids. They threw fireballs at the Keepers, who backed out of the room slowly, one of them looking right at Phillip. Phillip hit the big red button on the doors and ran to the rest of the teens.

"It's open!" Emery yelled from atop the table.

Phillip ran over by her, reached his hand out to help her down, but she ignored it and jumped down, and they saw the Keepers returning in special gray suits with large canisters. They put the canisters on the ground and started spraying white foam at the kids and the fire. The kids started running out the door, and Emery turned towards the Keepers. Phillip grabbed at her arm to run with them. She raised her hands into the air and back at the Keepers. The Keepers were all thrown back by a stream of fire, and Phillip stared in awe, and sudden incredible fear of the new situation he had decided to create in a moment.

"Come on, Emery." He said, grabbing her and pushing her out the door. Phillip looked back at the men on the ground and then forward at the group of kids running from the facility.

They kept running straight through the back of Camp Carce. There was a tower with a man who held some sort of a gun and sirens started going off. But the kids lit the tower on fire after one kid took a shot to the leg and fell to the ground. They ran through the woods for miles until kids started slowing down. Emery jogged towards the front of the group to find the boy with curly hair carrying two little kids as he jogged.

"Where are we going?" Emery asked.

"Far enough that they won't find us. We are a big group. That's not good for us. We need to avoid roads. They will catch us in the jeeps."

"But we also need to find our way. If we don't know where we are, we aren't safe either."

Emery looked behind at the frightened and tired kids and continued, "and they need rest."

The boy stopped jogging and walked with Emery, slowing everyone down.

"It's not safe." He said while letting one of the kids down and softly tickling the back of the other as they started crying again.

"Nowhere is safe anymore, but they are in our territory now." Emery said, pointing to the woods. "They could contain us in their steel cold camp. But here? In the forest that could be lit aflame in an instant? I think we should take a break. The more we plan here, the better off we are."

He looked at Emery. He hadn't noticed her much before. But something in her eyes made him trust her, and something in her looks gave him goosebumps.

"Ok."

He looked back at the group. "Break!"

All the kids sighed with relief and collapsed to the ground or nearby rocks. Emery and the mysterious boy whose name she would know forever quite soon took seats on a fallen tree. He set down the final kid he was carrying, he was maybe only three years old, and he went running to sit with the other two toddlers that were huddled with the rest of the teenagers. No one had thought to grab water, and they all needed it.

Emery looked at the kids, then Phillip climbed up the incline and stood in front of the curly hair boy and Emery. "We can't stay here."

"I know, but we also have exhausted kids and no water and no clue where we are," Emery said in a now tired voice.

"I'm going to scout out where we are." The boy with curly hair said.

"I had someone helping me. They told me we are in the northern mountains, and we should find a cabin. These aren't the deep woods. We have a chance if we head in the right direction. I've spent half my life camping with my dads and their friends. Let me go. You boys stay here and watch the children."

"Let me go with you," Phillip said.

"I'll protect the children." The curly hair boy said. Philip looked at him from the side of his eyes. He found himself annoyed at how this guy, who wasn't even trying, still sounded like a better person than him.

"I'm Emery. We haven't met." She put her hand out.

"Jasper." and when his hand slipped into hers to shake it, it somehow felt like a kiss.

"Ok, we don't have much time," Phillip said, pulling at Emery like a child. She paused and noticed a girl just a bit younger than her in front of them, with scrunchies on her wrist. She walked over to her and asked her for one.

Emery flipped her hair over and put it in a ponytail as she and Phillip began jogging further up the mountain. They weren't too far from the top, and both paused once they reached it. They looked down in both directions. Behind them, they could still see the camp. It was a distance, but it seemed to threaten them with unheard words.

"We are too close," Emery said, turning the other way around.

"There is a road down there." Phillip pointed.

"One better- look at that white roof. It's a cabin." She smiled, "That's it, we have to get there. Who knows what we could find!" She started jogging back down the mountain without once checking if Phillip was behind her.

When they made it back to the kids, she stood on a large log to speak to them.

"Everyone, I know you're scared. But we have some celebrations to be had as well. We aren't at Camp Carce anymore, but we still have a long journey to safety, and I need us all to keep being strong. There is more good news. I see a cabin. We have to get up this mountain, and it's a little farther down. This won't be a good place. We are still too close. But it's a place to regain our footing. We can get water, maybe food, maybe orient ourselves a bit." The kids all started talking at once, and Emery just hopped off the log and started walking. Looking behind her, and feeling content to see that they all got up and were now following her up the mountain, even through their conversations.

She couldn't help but notice Jasper falling behind and checking on the kids. Whenever one was getting tired, he would fall behind and walk with them. When two middle boys, maybe 12, started to cry from carrying their friend with the hurt leg, Jasper ran back to meet them. He started carrying the boy on his back, talking to him the whole time about when he was young and would hike with his friends. And this was all while Phillip was staring at Emery, trying to determine if he was capable of human emotions. All while Emery looked at Jasper and wondered if this was how she was supposed to feel, hot and confused. All while Jasper looked at another middle schooler, who was not watching where he was walking at all, wondering if he would be capable of carrying two middle schoolers at once.

When they arrived at the cabin, all the teens circled up in front of it. "Let's keep the kids behind while we check it out," said a girl named Emily, who had faded green hair and a septum piercing.

"Great," Emery added. "Make sure no one is home. If they are... don't start any fires just yet. Once they see smoke, they will have found us. Just yell if you see anyone. Don't take any chances." She said as she pointed in the direction they had come from.

The seven of the older teens, all together, circled the house, looking for entrances or to see if anyone was home. Meanwhile, they had the toddlers and middles wait behind in the trees. The cabin was white all around. It was small and one story with maybe a few bedrooms. It was surrounded by windows and felt dangerously quiet. There was a wrap-around porch with two old brown chairs in the front. It didn't look like a home. Everything was off and put away.

As Emery looked out from the porch, she spotted what looked like a car under a tarp. Then she heard Emily again, "All clear?"

All of the teens came together on the house's side in front of where the other kids were hiding. "All clear." They all agreed in the group.

Before anyone could come up with their next plan, she heard a bunch of glass breaking all at once. All of the teen's hands burst in flames, and Emery's burnt noticeably brighter and higher. Phillip put his head around the deck.

"I got us a way in."

"What the fuck?" Jasper interjected, startled enough that he dropped his flames and had to stomp them out with his foot.

They walked around to the front of the house to see that Phillip had thrown one of the chairs on the deck through the window. Phillip noticed the dirty looks and responded by crawling into the house and opening the door. Jasper nudged Emery and pointed to the kids, and they went into the woods to guide the kids into the cabin.

They all got into the cabin and found a simply decorated home covered in forest green. The kids started running around the house and playing with everything they could. Emery went to the kitchen first to see what food and water they had to begin planning what they should do next. Jasper walked into the kitchen and started looking through the cupboards as well. Emery watched him as he looked, not quite trusting this boy she didn't know.

They grabbed some chips and returned to the living room, where the small kids played with different things they had found like a puzzle and a wildlife book. Jasper noticed one of them was playing with a picture frame. Having grown up with five younger siblings, he knew to take anything glass from them immediately. He did this while remembering the time his little sister played with a lamp and broke it, which then led to 5 hours at the emergency room.

He pulled the frame from the kids and replaced it with a pillow from the couch. As he pulled it, he flipped it around to see the picture.

The picture itself wasn't scary. It was quite normal looking. It had a small family at some sort of party as rainbow-colored balloons hovered behind the family. Two small children were in their parents' hands, and one woman stood in the middle without any children and not touching anyone else in the photo. It was merely the fact that the woman in the middle was none other than Estrella, who stood awkwardly in the middle that was so disturbing.

"Guys, we have to find a new place to go." Jasper said, showing everyone the picture and passing it around to the other teens in the room. Once the picture got to Emery, she couldn't help but to study the picture of this woman. Something in her felt drawn to Estrella, and something about her made Emery feel she needed to know her more.

"We have to figure out exactly where we are." Emily said, nudging another teen named Kain who was tall and skinny with a yellow beanie. Emery studied the picture more before Phillip put his hand out to take it from her.

"We all need to search the house. Find camping materials, find maps, find anything we can use. Meet back here with what you found. We need to be gone by the morning." Emery added.

The kids and teens ran off in different directions and pulled the cabin apart. Where they were gentle and wary when they first entered the cabin, they now were destructive. Some of the kids seemed to be taking their anger for Estrella out on her things around the house. Emery, who I continue to follow because she is the most interesting, searched through the woman's closet upstairs. Jasper also followed her and also because she was the most interesting.

She looked through the Estrella's mostly black clothes and looked in each pocket. Part of her was only doing this because she was curious about who she was. But she was also looking for keys. She remembered what looked like a covered-up car out front and thought it could be their way out. She was do-ing five things at once. She was investigating a strange woman, planning for what to do if they got the car started, considering where they could go that was safe, wondering how she could use her power, growing concerned about all the kids and who was capable of what.

Emery did not find any keys. When she turned around, she bumped right into Jasper. It was a firm bump, and she blushed from it. He smiled at her.

"Not much up here. I looked through the drawers and found this, though." He said, revealing a black gun. Emery hadn't seen many guns in her life. She remembered her dad's friend Dale who also had his own cabin in the woods, and she and her dads had watched him shoot it into an abandoned mountain. It scared her, and she started crying, and he had put it away, and she never saw it again.

"Where was it?" Emery asked.

"In that top drawer."

"Leave it."

"What do you mean, leave it? Do you not remember us all being imprisoned a moment ago? Do you not remember that they will kill us in an instant if they see us? They kill kids like us, Emery."

"We don't need it. This is dangerous enough without a gun."

"It's dangerous enough with one too." He said, quickly losing the attraction he had for Emery in the first place be-cause that's how fragile affection can be.

"Put it back."

He rolled his eyes and returned the gun to the dresser, and Emery watched him as he hid it under some clothes.

"Look what I found!" they both heard someone shout from downstairs. Emery confirmed with Jasper through a silent moment that they would move on from this moment. Then they both started running down the stairs.

A middle school-aged boy named Jose had located all the camping gear. All the other middle school-age kids were bringing more gear in. He stood above two tents, one backpack, and some cooking material, looking proud.

Phillip stood above them, jealous. He noticed that Emery came down the stairs with Jasper, and he didn't like that at all. If we are honest, he also was jealous of young Jose, who had found something more useful than Phillip had. He wanted to tell Emery what he did. He wanted desperately to tell her that without him, they wouldn't have escaped. That he risked his own life to set them all free. But instead, he swept in his thoughts and decided to impress her another way.

He walked right out the front door. All the kids started searching through the materials, and Emily pulled a map from the backpack. "Love's Peak." She read. Emery walked over and looked at the map with her. Emery felt that fate had for once been on her side. The cabin that Dale owned was not far from Love's Peak. She knew the address by heart because she loved drawing a picture for family friends and sending them in the mail and because her dads brought her there so often. She grabbed a piece of paper from a notebook at the side of the couch and wrote the address down.

Then there was a honk from a car that made her

accidentally burn the paper in her hands. She jumped and ran outside while yelling at the other children to stay inside. Jasper, Emily, Emery, and another girl who hadn't said much ran out front. Two of four of them already with fire resting uneasily in their hands.

They found Phillip sitting in the front seat of the car that was now running and had been pulled out the front of the cabin. Emery was growing quite tired of Phillip and his seemingly sporadic behavior. But she felt relieved that this truck might provide them with some freedom. She walked up to it and put her head in the window. She saw that Phillip had torn out the wires on the driver's side and hot-wired the car.

"Don't think I'm not grateful. But, how exactly did you know how to do this?"

"You're asking the wrong questions, Emery. How can we use this?"

"I think I know. Come on inside."

They all went back inside, and some of their hands glowed red from the fires that had started from the fear of the car honking. Emery grabbed two pieces of paper and wrote the address to Dale's cabin on each.

"I think I know of a place we can go. It's already dark. I think we should rest tonight and leave in the morning. But this is the address of a cabin I know of that I think must be near. I'll spend tonight using the map to figure out a better direction as you all are sleeping."

"We will help," Jasper interjected. Emery didn't make eye contact.

"Kids, I think you should all find somewhere to sleep. Eat some snacks from the kitchen and be ready to move in the morning. Some of us will have to hike our way there, and we will have to find out who." Emery said facing everyone else.

The kids ignored this last directive, and all began playing again until they individually started falling asleep in the living room where they were playing. The teens stayed up in the kitchen, looking at the map and determining how they could draw a map to the new location that wasn't quite covered on the map that they had.

They whispered their plans so as not to wake up the kids. Emily stopped them all.

"Shhh," she said as her hands turned a bit red suddenly as she stuck them out. Then they all heard it, the quiet hum of a car approaching. The teens went off in different directions. Phillip ran after Emery, who ran out front and peeked around the porch. Emily and the quiet girl ran to the living room and started quietly waking up the children. Jasper and another teen named Kain ran upstairs to look through the windows, Jasper silently remembering they had another dangerous option lying in a drawer nearby.

Emery peered around and saw the black jeep approaching. She looked at Phillip.

"Get the car started." Phillip jumped off the porch and started the truck that was still out front. She ran inside the cabin.

"Middle school children and teens gather gear and fast! Be prepared to run. Follow me. Use your fire if you need to but be careful. We are in the woods, and even we can't survive a forest fire. Guys load the small children into the truck. We need to drive them away."

They ran out front, and the teens all lifted the small children into the back of the truck as the other car's lights were starting to come into view from around a bend.

"Emily, go with Phillip," Emery said, handing them the address and one of the maps they drew. "We will meet you there." Phillip wanted to protest as he didn't imagine showing them he could start the truck would end with carrying a bunch of small children and not being with Emery, but it all happened too fast and he was too worried about getting himself out of there safely. The truck drove down the road and swerved around the large black jeep. But the jeep didn't stop because it saw a flash of light towards the cabin.

What the jeep saw as it arrived in the cabin was a fire. Emery was standing in front as Jasper and Kain led the children into the woods. Emery stood with fire in her hands. She drew a thin line of flame on the dirt ground in front of them. One Keeper and Estrella came out of the jeep quickly, and with surprise, like they hadn't intended to find the children here.

Estrella stood back and looked at Emery. She knew what Emery was capable of and wasn't prepared for this fight. So they stood and stared at her. Emery couldn't take any chance with power like a gust of wind. She threw flames at the car, and as the car exploded, she ran with the older kids and Jasper into the woods.

8

The Lost

Those scared kids were on the run for about an hour. Every 30 minutes or so, they changed directions in case they were being followed. All together now, 11 kids were running through the woods. Five teenagers remained, Emery, Jasper, Kain, the girl she hadn't spoken to yet, and Gish, another girl who spent most of her time muttering things to herself. The rest were a bit younger. But all the youngest kids were now with Phillip and Emily in the car.

Emery was thinking about this a lot while running, how they had trusted Phillip and Emily with the most innocent and most fragile children. She knew this choice meant they had a better chance of getting away. But she didn't trust Phillip, and she didn't trust Emily. She, of course, was right not to trust Phillip. The worst thing that can happen is when someone has faulty logic but ends up being right all along anyway. Her fear of trusting people was becoming a hole she dug into everyday, and would never fill back up.

The kids ran and sometimes walked until it began to grow dark again. The girl Emery hadn't met yet sat next to

Emery and drank some water they had filtered out from a nearby river.

"I'm Macy."

"Emery," she said, handing her the water.

Macy pulled out the maps she had been put in charge of, not because Emery felt this girl knew maps. But only because she had no choice but to use the few teens they had in their group for any job that would come up along their journey. They would all need to pretend to be experts, as Emery felt like she was pretending to be a leader.

Macy had gray hair that was wild and wavy. She pulled it into a tight ponytail that had the curls reaching out almost as if for help.

"I've been looking at this quite a bit. We have been walking for a while. I was a girl scout my whole life. I grew up camping and looking at maps."

Something about Macy saying this made Emery feel bad for not wanting this girl to be in charge of the map, for not trusting her in the same way she would never quite trust herself.

"I think we went the wrong way a bit. We are too far east. In the morning, we need to move mostly west. If we did that, we could be at this cabin this time tomorrow. If we keep moving, then maybe even earlier."

Emery took the map and didn't realize that it looked a bit rude.

"Thanks, Macy, that's helpful. We only have two tents. I think we should stay out, and we can trade off being on watch. There is a blanket we can set up next to the fire we are building. Then we can take shifts getting a little rest."

She looked back and saw Jasper teaching the younger group of kids to start a fire. It was a sweet moment that gave a small taste of the sweetness that was really in him. But, also, Emery couldn't help but think that it didn't seem like the time or place and was slightly relieved when one of the boys pointed his finger and flames flew out of it to start the fire. It did seem like the one skill these kids would never need.

She saw a younger girl off on her own to the side, almost wandering out of sight. Emery got up and walked towards her. She was wearing a bright pink shirt and blue jeans. She had large round glasses and blonde hair that looked dirty, but not the color. No, it just actually looked dirty. She was searching on the ground and moving somewhat quickly. The little girl wore pigtails, and Emery immediately thought of the young girl Estrella had had in the study room and wished that that girl had escaped with all of them and wondered how many more kids she needed to save. She walked up to the little girl searching the ground.

"What ya looking for?" Emery asked.

"I wanted to find good places for everyone to sit."

"Well, that's a very nice idea. Can I help?"

"Sure! Look for a flat surface big enough for a butt." She said, motioning with her hands.

"Got it. I'm Emery. What's your name?"

"Dalila. Look, I found one." She said, pointing to a part of a far too heavy tree for her to lift. She looked at Emery sadly. She felt bad that this cool older girl had come to talk to her, and she wouldn't help get the log over to the group. Emery smiled, grabbed the log, and walked it over to where the other children were now standing, admiring the fire they had just built. She noticed Jasper was already over setting up the tents. She also felt something strange in her fingers when she noticed he was laughing with Macy while doing it.

She felt struck by this feeling. It terrified her. She looked at her hands and saw them glowing slightly with the red tint. She remembered what happened the last time she felt jealousy. She was so busy trying to escape her kidnapping that she did not take enough time with what happened directly before the kidnapping. The fire at the bowling alley. She must have started the fire when she got jealous.

She desired a moment to run away. She wanted to turn herself in and make sure there were consequences for her actions. But, looking at the other kids, she knew that she had no other choice but to put these feelings on pause. She would need to use her abilities to make sure they were all safe first, and then she could begin to consider what she would do and who she would be.

Once the camp was all set up, the kids all joined around the fire and just relaxed for the first time since their kidnapping. Emery enjoyed the interaction on a different level than the rest. She hadn't had this sort of interaction with other teens before. She slowly began to realize that this was intentional. Her dads knew of her abilities and were preventing this exact outcome.

As the night settled and only Emery and Macy remained

at the fire. Macy was getting tired, and Emery kept a lookout for strange noises. Which when you are in the woods, there is never a shortage of. The woods' noises feel so foreign and dangerous in the beautiful silence that they sent shivers up Emery's spine every couple of moments.

The morning came soon enough though, and with the first light, the group packed up everything they needed. They walked all day mostly in silence, as their joy from the evening before had transformed into determination to arrive some-where/anywhere safe.

After a day of walking, the relief at the sight of the cabin Emery recognized was overwhelming. The dark wood cabin could be seen above the woods a bit. There were large spiral stairs leading up to the front door. But the relief of the sight of the cabin could not overpower the fear she felt. The truck wasn't there.

The teens dropped everything in front of the cabin and celebrated. Some of them were laughing and shoving each other, some of them were crying. But Emery looked at Jasper.

"The truck." She said.

"Maybe they left to get supplies. Let's look around and see if they got in." Jasper replied.

The two walked around the cabin to look for ways to get inside. But they didn't find any broken windows, open doors, or other signs of the other children. Emery made one more lap, this time she ran in a panic, then made her way to the front with Jasper again. They stood in front of the front door in absolute fear and a short moment of silence that felt neverending. They looked into each other's eyes.

"It doesn't look like they have been here," Emery whispered.

"Ok, maybe they stopped on their way to get supplies. I would have done the same. Let's give them some time." he said while lightly putting his hand on her arm for a slight second.

"And then what? How would we even find those little kids?"

"One thing at a time, Emery. We can only ever put out one fire at a time."

Emery walked to the side of the house and saw some kids about to throw a chair through the window, as Phillip did at the last cabin. She stopped them by putting her hands up and they glowed red like they had during her battles at Camp Carce.

"Wait, wait. Let's do this softer. Go grab something smaller, and let's break it just enough so we can reach in and open the window." She bent down towards them. "Then it will be easier to cover, and how fun would it be for one of you to climb into the window and let us all in!"

One of the boys ran down and came back with a rock. She let the boys break the glass and open the window. Then they played rock paper scissors to decide who got to climb in the window.

Once all of the kids got into the cabin, they found corners and beds they would share and would be their own space. The cabin was somewhat large. It had three bedrooms on the main level, with bunk beds in two of them. One master bedroom upstairs had its own door, which was snagged by the group of girls who were a bit younger.

Emery was happy with a small recliner in the living room

and decided that this would be the best place she could listen for visitors or, more importantly, the missing truck. Everyone fell asleep rather quickly after the past two days of running. Emery surprised herself when she did too. She was also surprised when she woke up in the middle of the night to see Jasper blocking off the broken window with a couple different logs of wood he was binding together.

She fell back asleep quickly in the foreign comfort she felt in him, making sure they were safe. She was the first to rise, though, and she immediately started looking for food. Since the cabin was only used for vacation, she was not surprised that she didn't find very many food options. There were about ten cans of food. She cooked two of the spaghetti-os cans and put out dishes for all the kids to fill and eat.

Once all the kids were settled, eating breakfast in their beds and their corners. The older teens all sat down at the main table together.

"We need food," Emery said

"We need the truck. Where are they?" Macy added.

"I don't know." Jasper continued. "But the first step has to be food. Emery, do you know where the nearest store is?"

"We don't have any money."

"Let me contact my dads. They helped us escape Camp Carce."

Jasper looked skeptical. "Camp Carce is probably watching them very closely right now. You could put us all in danger."

"We don't have very many options," Emery said.

Macy played with her food and said, "We aren't using our resources." She said as she lit a flame within her hands.

"We shouldn't," Emery said, putting her hands out to hers.

"We have to. This is what we were meant for. Ignoring it is not only irresponsible but disrespectful to the universe or gods that gave it to us. Where is the store? I'll start a distraction. You guys go in and grab food."

Jasper looked to Emery, "Normally, I'd agree with you. But we have to eat. We have to feed them."

Emery didn't look back at him and instead held intense eye contact with Macy, who, just like that, she no longer trusted.

"Once. Then we need to plan for something more sustainable. We also can't spend our lives running from Camp Carce. We need to make sure they aren't kidnapping more kids. But we need to do all of this with grace. Otherwise, if we are a danger to society. Maybe we deserve to be there." A heavy silence fell before she continued. "The store is only 30 minutes away. I don't know the directions for sure, but I saw a whole shelf of maps earlier. Let's plan the trip and leave by afternoon, so we are back by the evening. Hopefully, the truck will be here by then. If not, I'm going to leave to find them."

Before the older teens headed for the store, they gathered all the kids in the living room. They reminded them that they were all still in danger.

Jasper spoke with a deep and clear voice, "You have to remember that your power is dangerous. Fire spreads fast, and it can kill." he paused, "But use it if you're in danger. Do what it takes to protect yourself but nothing more." The kids acted quite uninterested and unphased. But inside, they were scared and still children.

The teens made the journey to a small little corner store

and gas station. Emery forgot that it was a gas station as well and worried more about Macy's ability to control herself. She stopped Macy, Kain, and Jasper right before they got there,

"Wait, maybe I should create the distraction," Emery said, and Macy kept walking.

"Emery, you've done enough deciding, and I want to make it very clear that you aren't in charge. Hold back while I distract." Emery wished in that moment that Macy hadn't begun to open up so much and that she returned to the quiet Macy that first escaped with them.

Macy walked around to the back of the store as Jasper and Emery hid behind the gas pump, waiting for the go-ahead. Kain was even further back watching the area to make sure he didn't see any ominous black jeeps come by, or worse, head to get gas.

Nothing about this plan was subtle or safe, as Emery feared. A tree maybe 50 feet from the station behind it went up in flames. They heard Macy scream, "Fire ! Help!" as she ran by the station, then kept running past Jasper and Emery back in the woods' direction. An older man in overalls and a lady in a denim blue dress ran out of the store. They pulled at the hose, and the man started spraying the tree as the woman watched and called 911, and cried silently fearing for the nature that she called home.

Jasper and Emery took the small moment and ran into the store. They stuffed as much food as they could in their backpacks and ran out just in time for the old woman to turn and see just their backsides running back into the woods. Jasper kept running and only looked back once to find that Emery was not running with him. He turned back around and found Emery watching the older couple fight the fire from the woods.

"What are you doing? We have to go."

"We have to help them."

"It's going down. They will be fine."

She handed him her backpack full of food.

"You can take the food, Jasper. I am waiting here until I know the fire went out, and the couple is ok."

Jasper set both backpacks down and perched next to Emery without saying a word. It was kind. It almost made Emery feel bad for holding secrets. When they ran through the store, she saw a cell phone by the front desk and had quickly tucked it into her bra. Something told her that what she would choose to do with this phone needed to be only her decision. They only left when they saw the fire was out, and the older couple had returned safely to their posts.

When they got back to the cabin, they found everyone circled around another massive fire and Macy laughing and telling them all what happened. Emery was not prone to violence. She wasn't prone to losing her temper. But, she was losing it. She ran up yelling.

"What are you guys doing?" She pointed to Dalila and a couple of other kids. "Go get jugs of water." Then she turned in front of Macy. Her anger was suddenly revealing flames that ran in lines straight down her arms. She looked down and backed away. She put her back towards the kids as Jasper helped the younger kids put the fire out, and she calmed herself down. Once her arms were no longer in flames, she walked straight up to Macy again.

"This isn't a game, Macy."

"I'm not making it a game. But we have to use what we have to survive."

"We have to control what we have to survive."

"We were just celebrating."

"Celebrating what?"

"Your little buddy Dalila stole a laptop from Estrella's, and the kids hooked it up to the internet here."

"That's great news," Emery said, smiling at Dalilah. "But this isn't how we celebrate, and it's dangerous."

Kain quietly added. "It seems like you're the most dangerous one of all of us."

9

Once Upon A Time

Emery had a plan. She would destroy the laptop and connect her phone to the internet instead. She knew it was selfish. She knew it was possibly dangerous. But she was surrounded by kids that she didn't know. Anything they did, anything they said, would mean the fate of other children. She just couldn't risk people's lives by trusting other people.

She only knew of two people she could trust, and she would do everything she could to contact them. She knew her dads must be worried sick. But she was also not as dumb as most people are. No. She knew that contacting her dads was a serious risk. Not only to the children she was with, because they could be tracked, but mostly to her dads.

She stayed up at night thinking about it. Only a few of the older kids were still up out back laughing and sharing some beers they had found in the cabin. Emery stared at the sleeping children and decided that she would risk her family's safety in hopes of finding a better solution for these children, to find the lost children and rescue the kids in Camp Carce. She would need their help.

So she quietly got up and left out the front door so as not

to be noticed. She slowly closed it, and the slight creak it made felt loud and dangerous. If you have ever snuck out of somewhere, you know that every breath, every creek, is a threat to the entire mission.

But she snuck out unseen and unheard, or so she thought. She walked down the stairs and felt relieved by how loud the teens in the back were being. She still walked pretty far into the woods as she kept her eye on the cellphone's phone service. She had quite a few things to juggle right now. She wanted to go far enough that people would not be able to hear her speak, not so far that she wouldn't have service, far enough that she felt safe, not so far that she couldn't find her way back.

Creeping step by step into the woods felt strangely relieving. There was a part of her that just wanted to keep walking forever. She wanted to go forward and forget all these newfound responsibilities. Something about the woods whispered to her to come deeper. Once she was deeper in them, the woods whispered to stay. To rest. To quit. She stopped walking and felt so lured in by the woods that in a moment of awe, of dreadful peace, she dropped the phone to the ground, and it blended with the almost pitch black ground.

She knelt and started feeling around for it. Then she stood up, looked at her hands, and took a breath. She put out one finger. She didn't want to start a fire. She only wanted to light it. To her surprise, as she thought it, a small and caring flame sprouted from her fingertip. She smiled at her new companion. I even thought I saw tears of love fill her eyes.

But she shook her whole body to rid herself of them and moved the light to the ground to find the phone. She grabbed it and pulled it up. She decided to call her pa's phone since she knew her dad was more likely being watched than her pa. She dialed the number and stalled a moment before pressing the call button.

It rang, and her heart felt like it was beating again.

"Heller?"

She hadn't planned very well for this occasion. She wanted to cry and ask her Pa for help. But she pictured Camp Carce listening in. she had to be as discreet as possible.

"Hi, this is Danni from work."

Her dads always said that they wanted to name a child Danni one day, and she knew it wasn't even necessary because he would know her voice. He would know what was happening. There was a pause, and silence fell, then a slight noise like a small cough. Pa's voice had changed a bit and sounded weaker than it was when he answered.

"Danni," a pause of silence that somehow said I love you, then he continued.

"Can you hold for a moment? I imagine this is about Tuesday's meeting. I'm going to get a notepad and put you on speaker so that I can take notes."

"Sure."

"Ok, I have you. Good to go. Do we have a safe location for Tuesday's meeting?"

"For now, we do. But the meeting space could change at any moment."

"I have an idea for a safer, more stable place."

There was an awkward pause. I think they both realized that words needed to be said. Plans needed to be made, and there was only so far they could go without being blunter with each other. Like daughter, like father, they both gave up at the same time. Her Pa's voice changed into low and stern.

"We love you.... Danni... just wanted you to know because I know that you've been having issues at home."

"I love you guys." She said, letting tears flow down her cheeks but not wiping them away because the woods wouldn't judge her.

"This is important. Remember the story of the witches. They are safe. Be safe."

This was going to change everything. Emery's life would not be the same after this. When Emery was young, her dads would always read her two stories at bedtime. One would be a book of her choice. But, one story, one story was the same every single night—the story of the harmless witches.

She pictured being cuddled in the middle of her dads as they told the story night after night after night.

Once upon a time, there was a group of harmless witches. These poor witches didn't even know about their power until it was too late. They were truly harmless! When they discovered they had powers, they only used them to make elaborate plays, clean the home, and make music. It was all truly harmless! But bad people found out about the witches.

A wicked woman who was deeply jealous of their powers wanted to do everything she could to take it from them. She kidnapped other witches before and kept them all in small dungeons where they couldn't use their powers anymore. The witches were so sad in the dungeons, unable to have any fun or enjoy their new powers anymore.

The truly harmless witches knew the woman was coming this time, though. Another witch had told them she was coming. They gathered up all their stuff and ran. They could have fought her. Of course, they could have fought her. But these witches were truly harmless. So instead, they ran. But they didn't just run. They made it so they would never have to run again.

They built themselves a secret home that was hidden in the woods. The entrance was hidden deep in the woods and looked like a small fragile misplaced diner. There would occasionally be a confused customer who would wander in. They would feed them and go. But in the diner's deep back was the entrance to a large building where the witches could live, use their magic, and be safe.

This was the home of the harmless witches. When another harmless witch was scared of bad people, they would always know. Go to Penotia Pass. Find the lake with the bluest waters. Walk west until your feet hurt. Take the small bridge, then to the right until your legs hurt. There any harmless witch would be safe, and that's what all people of all types deserve.

Emery quickly realized what her Pa was saying. She quickly understood why they spent so many nights telling her the same story over and over again. When she got older and was too young to hear the story, they would have her tell the story to her little cousin. "Tell her the story of the harmless witches!" Her Dad would always push.

She also knew that if Camp Carce was listening in on this phone call, their cover was blown. She was not sure how casual it could look that he told his coworker how much he loved her and remembered a story about witches. She tried quickly to save it.

"Yes, what a silly story to bring up. I agree, just like in that story. The best place would be somewhere well lit. Good thinking, I'll change the meeting spot to the downtown library."

She wasn't sure what to say next or what she needed next. She had one million questions and a thousand more whines to tell her dads. She knew she couldn't say any of it. But she also didn't want to hang up. If she could just leave the phone on to her home constantly and go about her business, she would. She felt grateful they had taught her where to go to find safety, but the reality was, only her dads really made her feel safe.

"We will see you again," Pa said.

"We will win." Her Dad's voice was added, and the simple words gave her hope. Just hearing his voice gave her renewed strength.

"We will leave now, and we will find you. This conversation is just the beginning. We have to go. Stay strong baby girl."

"I love you guys," Emery said, choking up a bit now, and the phone abruptly hung up, unexpectedly, before she even got her sentence completely out.

When Emery woke up the next morning, she knew what she was going to do. She had a complete plan and only now realized she wouldn't be able to do it alone. She wished that the kids would all just believe her, that they would follow her into the unknown. But she now realized that she just didn't have the power. So, when she noticed Jasper go outside early in the morning with some coffee, she followed him.

She was nervous to talk to him. But it wasn't because of her plan. It was because she was beginning to feel something quite foreign whenever she was with him. She remembered, of course, her first date, and the picture of her date in the fire was enough to stifle out any emotions that were stirring.

When she walked outside, she found Jasper, sitting on the stairs drinking his coffee. She went and sat next to him. Silently, he handed her his coffee.

"I'm ok, thank you."

He took the coffee back and kept drinking.

"What's next?" He said without making eye contact, just staring ahead still.

"I have a plan. I wanted to chat with you about it."

He then turned his head and looked into her eyes deeply. He just stared into her eyes. He even noticed the hazel in them that only her dads had noticed before. Emery couldn't think of a time she felt more uncomfortable, and she was only able to hold eye contact for about five seconds before she put her head down and started playing with the wood on the stair as she spoke.

"I know of a place that my parents taught me is a safe place for people like us. I think we should take this group there."

"What about the kids with Phillip and Emily?"

Emery didn't bring that part up because she needed Jasper's help to get this group safely. But she wasn't planning on taking him with her to find the children. But she realized that Jasper was, in fact, smarter than she once thought he was.

"I'm going to find them after everyone is safe."

He chuckled, and his deep laugh made her all the more

uncomfortable. She noticed these deep dimples cut holes into his cheek and her heart simultaneously.

"We." He said, putting his hand gently on her back for just a moment. But, after he moved it, the absence of it suddenly felt like it was a ghost touch that she couldn't remove.

"Sure, we can find them. I'm going to start with Camp Carce, though. It's the only place I can think of. I can only imagine that the Keepers caught them at some point. It works anyway because I was planning on returning anyway to free the other children at that camp."

"Ambitious." He smiled, and the dimples called to Emery again. "I like it."

"Well, first, we need to get this group to a safe place. It's about an hour away if we drive, according to my calculations."

"We can leave early in the morning and be there by the evening if we backpack there."

Emery's confidence slightly returned as she looked him in the eyes.

"We should leave today. I have to get to those other kids."

"You sure do love the word I."

"Sorry." She twirled a part of her hair, and she wasn't quite sure what emotion she was feeling anymore.

"I see your rush, though." He sipped the last of his coffee in confidence. "Let's give everyone a little time to wake up, and then we can let them know."

Emery stood up, satisfied with the awkward success.

"I'm going to start getting ready. Packing up anything that might be useful for us."

With that, she walked down the stairs to begin inspecting

what tools or resources they had in the small storage under the stairs.

When Jasper came to find Emery to help him tell the kids what was happening, she already had a couple of bags out front and ready to go. She sang as she packed and was mortified when Jasper started clapping after her song. She jumped.

"Sorry, I didn't mean to scare you. I gathered everyone in the living room so we can give them the plan."

Emery set down the shovel she was wrapping up to pack for the journey.

"I don't think we should tell them about returning to Camp Carce. I don't want to put any of them in danger. I just want to get them to a safe place."

"Well, look at that. Me and the mysterious beauty agreed."

She felt something in her stomach that made her uncomfortable when he called her a beauty. At first, it felt like butterflies. But these butterflies were aggressive. They flew like they were on fire, and it made Emery feel a bit like puking. She combatted this by walking as aggressively as the butterflies right past him.

They entered the room, and all the kids were talking and laughing loudly. Emery didn't feel like it was the time for joy, butterflies, or happiness of any sort. She would only indulge in that sort of behavior once she knew everyone was safe.

She stood in front of them, and Jasper came next to her, but stood slightly behind her.

"Alright, guys." No one listened, and she couldn't tell for sure, but it felt like they actually got even louder. "I think we should," she said even more quietly than the first time. Jasper slightly smirked at her.

Then there was a fire.

Macy set a book on fire and held it in her hands as it was aflame. Everyone looked at her and giggled, an innocent giggle becoming more and more unlike the truth every day.

"Guys, I think Emery has something to say." She said calmly.

Jasper walked over and grabbed the book out of her hands. Everyone watched, looking for the details. They noticed it didn't burn his hand as he took it from her. He threw it in the fireplace, and everyone began making calculations in their head. The kids didn't know very much about their powers. Some of them were in Camp Carce before they even knew they had them. Each small thing they witnessed about the power they internalized with panic. Their lives were certainly not the same anymore. Their natural instinct had them all preparing with how to survive. The silence spoke volumes about their uncertainty. Until Emery broke it sharply with a voice of authority, she wasn't aware existed in her.

10

Finding Adults

"Ok." Emery looked to Macy and wanted to begin by telling her off, but she held it in instead. She controlled her focus and faced all the rest of the kids.

"I know we just got here. I know you feel safe. But the reality is it isn't safe. We don't even know where the other kids are. What if they told Camp Carce where we are? We need to move, and we need to move quickly." The room broke into conversation like she put in headphones of whining voices and questions. "I have good news, though!" She shouted over them, this time only to avoid Macy setting something on fire to get their attention.

"I know of a place. I was taught when I was younger about a safe place for people like us. It's hidden, but I have the directions, and we could walk there in under a day. I know you guys don't want to walk again. But we have to do what it takes to survive. If we make it to this place, the possibilities are endless. There will be other people like us. There will be adults to guard us and help us. "

Although this group of children would never admit it, they missed adults dearly. Even the children who came from bad homes missed their teachers. They all just missed the security of adults. It was something they only recently realized was how they were able to truly be kids. Kids who have to do all the adult work aren't really kids at all.

They all agreed to this glimpse of hope peeking through. Jasper began with the specifics.

"We are going to bring whatever might be helpful. Prepare to spend the night in the woods again, just in case. But grab what you need or what you think might be helpful. Teens grab all edible food and even non-edible food, just in case. We will head out in thirty minutes."

After a moment of chatter after the announcements, the kids all went to work. They almost tore apart the cabin looking for things. It felt like an extreme game of hide and seek. Just none of the children knew exactly what they were seeking. Emery packed food from the cabinet and turned around to see all the kids destroying the cabin. She felt extremely guilty and promised herself to replace anything they took and to one day fix up the cabin to even better shape.

She pictured her and her dads fixing up the cabin together. Joaquin would be in the corner putting the cabinets on tighter while Erick would be sweeping up the floor. They would all be laughing at the wild adventures that seemed as if they would never end. Towards the end of her daydream, she even thought that for a moment she saw Jasper doing the dishes out of her peripheral vision. But she snapped out of it as a book the kids were tearing threw flew by her face. When she returned to reality, she felt silly for the thought, and again bad for the state they were leaving Dale's cabin in. But she knew that sometimes the right things are disguised as bad things and that she was doing the right thing.

When they left, she found that destroying the cabin was only partly successful. The group all showed off what they found, like a distorted show and tell. While the lighters and gas that Gish found were helpful, her friend, a little boy named Eric, only found a whistle that could call deers. When Jose showed his find, Eric felt less bad about only finding a deck of cards. But Macy made up for that with the hunting knife that she found. Emery, who was growing untrustful of Macy, vowed mentally to steal the knife the first chance she got. She was finding that she wasn't only going to have to keep the kids safe from Camp Carce adults, but also, ultimately, from each other.

They all grabbed their stuff and left the cabin. They started following Jasper, who had a compass one of the middle schoolers found in the search. They were to head north for 45 minutes first. It would be a bit complicated, but they had studied the maps on the phone that she had only shared with Jasper in the secret meeting behind the cabin.

Emery stopped for a moment and turned around to look at the cabin. She thought to herself what she often thought when she left somewhere. She took a moment to breathe in the memory, to open the door that led to her soul, so it could forever be a part of her. She wasn't sure what kind of memory it was just yet. It could be the memory of the last time she felt unsafe. The memory where she got to know her soulmate, or maybe started hating her soulenemy. Maybe it was the memory of the last time she felt safe.

There were no certainties about the road ahead, with that no certainties of life in general. It could be the last memory she had of sleeping and waking up. All the possibilities were apparent, but more than that was the feeling that this memory was important, no matter what it held. After her breath, she turned around and saw Dalila also stopped and looked back at Emery, she jogged forward and motioned for her to come on with a smile.

The walk was harder than they anticipated. Sometimes the woods were unforgiving, and they had to take trails that took them the long way. But every child pushed on, and every child kept moving. When Emery noticed multiple children crying as she walked, she suggested they set up camp instead. It was a safe enough looking spot, and at this rate, they were going to be arriving in the night. She trusted her dads, and that they were headed to a safe place. But you can never be too careful, and bad luck arrives when you go anywhere at night. They weren't hard to convince, and kids were setting up sleeping areas before she had even finished her argument to the older teens.

When the sun started going down, Emery decided to handle the fire this time. She called Dalila over and had her practice starting the fire with her hands. Emery was not against using their power. She understood that it could be a gift. But she also deeply understood that sometimes the gifts wrapped in the nicest wrapping paper contain the most terrible gifts. She wouldn't be explaining this to Dalila just yet. So, she settled by telling her to only practice with Emery or an adult and that then she would be able to learn to use it for good.

It took a few moments of Dalila awkwardly throwing her hands towards the wood in a pile, while nothing happened. Emery put her arms around Delila and told her to focus on the feeling of warmth that has happened when she starts fires. Emery, at the same time, was practicing her own power, by practicing how to not start a fire on accident while she guided Dalila. They took a deep breath together and finally fire sprung from Dalila's hands. It was a small flame that barely reached the wood, but Dalila got so excited she immediately turned around to tell her friends, not noticing that it didn't actually start the fire. So Emery shot a ball of fire into the fire pit while she wasn't looking.

Dalila turned around and saw the fire she thought she created now raging beautifully. She ran off excitedly to those friends to now tell them all about what she did. Emery bent down and stuck her hand in the fire. She hadn't done this before. But recently, she had been thinking about how she never felt burned after the fire, just warm, and was becoming more and more curious by each day. She watched as the flame hugged her hand. Then, as her hand seemed to light aflame as well; and she was mesmerized by her small flame in the large fire.

"Cool, right?"

She jumped and pulled her hand out that was still aflame, and a piece of the flame hit the ground outside the fire pit. She stomped it out as she waved her hand out as well.

"Sorry!" Jasper said, putting his hands in the air as if surrendering, with a small smirk on her face.

Emery quickly cooled down. "It's ok. I just. You just scared me."

"It's cool, though, right?"

"I haven't quite decided the right word for it just yet." She paused, "But I don't think that the word is cool."

Now he bent down and looked at the fire. "I didn't know we couldn't be burned until I grabbed that book, you know?"

"Then why did you grab it?"

"Because of this." He leaned down and looked at the fire now crouched; he stuck his own hand in the fire for a moment. "It's so dangerous, Emery." He looked at her, and she felt like a child when he glanced at her. He stood back up and looked at the fire next to Emery and looked right in her eyes as he continued.

"It's cool. It's magic, really. But I can't think of many other powers that would be this dangerous." He looked back to the fire. "Especially with the amount that you have. I've seen it a couple of times. You have something different than us. We can start these flames like this." He put his hands out, only to feel the warmth of the fire now. "Flames that could start a small fire and grow into a dangerous large one if we aren't careful. But you. You can start the big dangerous ones like it's a match. I'm not quite sure about how I feel knowing that someone here has the power to burn everything with the simpleness of a flick." As he said this last part, he looked back at Emery, who was staring at him with what may have been persistent tears sitting casually in her eyes.

"I appreciate your concerns Jasper, and you're not alone in

them." She walked away before she accidentally revealed more about herself than she would like. Before she started crying from her own growing fear of herself. She walked off into the woods by herself to spend some time meditating, a habit her pa Erick had taught her. As the darkness grew she returned to the campsite with the other teens.

Emery sat by the fire next to Jasper. They spoke in whispers to not wake the other children. But it somehow made the conversation feel gentle, almost sexy, but she wasn't quite sure what that meant just yet. Jasper had occasionally gotten up to get wood, and every time he did when he returned, he sat a bit closer to Emery until she felt his leg touch her own in short waves as if he would notice the touching and move a bit and then would lightly allow them to touch again.

"I'm sorry I walked away earlier. I'm not always the best at revealing pieces of myself." She felt her hands grow a bit hot as she said this and noticed how her power seemed to be showing itself so much easier now that she was learning to use it.

"No, I totally understand. It wasn't my place to say those things to you. But I also just felt like I had to say it. Just once."

"I would have done the same." She reflected in the image of the flames. "No, I would have been so much more aggressive about it." She laughed a bit at herself. He looked at her, and she looked back as his whispered voice cut the air.

"You're beautiful."

Emery accidentally made a clearly shocked face when he said that. They both laughed a bit at the ridiculousness of her face. But Jasper noted that the girl he was beginning to fall for wasn't used to being called beautiful, and he vowed to change that. But first, he had a more pressing desire.

"Can I kiss you?"

Emery had dreamed about moments like this. She spent late nights picturing the perfect boy in every way. She imagined him looking a certain way and even holding her a certain way. She imagined showing him off to all the kids at school and them all crying at how wrong they were about her. She had even, and this is the whole truth, even imagined a perfect boy kissing her somewhere hidden in the woods.

"No," she said with panic in her eyes then she got up and went and laid down in the blanket. She laid out carefully on the edge of the group of camping kids.

She didn't sleep for a while, and instead, she wondered what exactly was wrong with her. She wished she could talk to her dads about it or that she had a friend she could talk to, but instead, she just lay there and thought about how she would never quite be like any of the other girls. She wondered if she had just said no to her first and last kiss, and most importantly, why, why was she so quick to say no to him?

At the same time, Jasper looked into the dark of the woods and wondered what was wrong with him. He wished that he had been smoother; he had waited; he had shown some more respect to the beautiful girl instead of letting his hormones jump like the flames in the fire. He wondered if he had just ruined his second and last kiss.

Emery ended up concluding that she was too scared. She was too scared to even like a boy again after what happened to Levi. It wasn't just the kissing of Eva. It was the fire and the danger of it all. If she was so incredibly dangerous, she shouldn't like anyone again, which she figured now would not be a problem, as she had so badly ruined any chances with Jasper.

Jasper, on the other hand, concluded quite the opposite. He concluded that this was only the beginning. That the no was just fine, it was better than fine. He understood that ultimately, they barely knew each other. She was clearly scared, and they were just trying to find a way to survive. It wasn't the right time to chase his whirlwind feelings. He would wait. He would be patient and hope that the next time she would be the one to ask him, but only when she was actually ready.

The next morning, the kids and teens were all grateful for their rest in the woods. As they rolled up their blankets, tents, and hammocks, they laughed and many of them reflected on how they would never be in this position again. You see, it's human nature to always see positives even in the very worst of times, and even the most negative of people have a light of hope in them that will never go out.

They headed to their new location with determination in each step. They cheered as they walked. Two kids with soft, harmonizing voices sang Hallelujah as they walked. The positive energy was so contagious Emery herself began to enjoy the walk. She smiled as they walked on and let herself live in this moment. She stopped making delightfully cunning plans in her head and just allowed herself to have this.

For a while, at least, until they saw a striking red chimney resting above the woods a bit. They all stopped and began walking with less purpose and more hesitance. Emery picked up her speed and stood at the front with the other teens. They walked in silence and only stopped again once a strange diner was in complete view.

The trees suddenly stopped, and a perfect circle filled with perfect grass surrounded the diner. In large and whimsical blue letters, it said, "His Place Diner" The diner itself was bright white with blue details on each corner and down each side. It looked like a fancy diner with a rustic theme that belonged in a secret corner of some big downtown city.

Emery looked to Jasper, and he looked back. It was the first looks they had exchanged since the denial of the kiss. It was like it hadn't happened. Emery somehow felt comfort in those eyes, and as if they had had a conversation without words, they nodded at each other as they walked in front and led the group through the large blue doors that were the entrance to the diner.

Bells rang through the diner as they opened the door and piled inside. The diner was, to their surprise, completely full. Children and adults of all ages filled the shiny and almost sparkling white booths. The tables shined as well, with deep wood that looked both rare and common at the same time. All of the chatter amongst all the tables stopped at once, and everyone stared at the teens and kids.

A woman with bright red hair in a high ponytail and a red apron walked towards the kids. Her heels clicked in the silence, echoing through the diner. The teens took every click as an opportunity to force themselves to breathe. She walked right up to Emery.

"And how might we be helping you youngins?"

"I don't. I don't quite know."

"Well, did y'all stop by for a meal? We've got scrambled eggs done Denver style as a special." She said with a look of suspicion on her face instead of genuine interest in their orders for food. It was hard to imagine many people looking for food would be wandering into this diner, but I've seen stranger things in my time, much stranger.

Dalila ran up and stood next to Emery while holding on to her arm as if she might fly away.

"We are from Camp Carce." Dalila said, feeling safer as long as she was holding on tightly to Emery.

The pretty woman with bright red hair looked down at her. Emery pushed Dalila a bit farther behind her, and Dalila let go as Emery now had her arm wrapping her behind her body, unsure what to expect, unsure how sure her dads knew that this was a safe place. For just a moment, she feared it could be another trap from Camp Carce itself.

The woman scooted back and looked back and forth at all the people dining. She looked around at all the teens and kids behind Emery, and then, quite unexpectedly, she smiled. A large goofy smile that showed her large white teeth.

"Everyone fire extinguish those flames. I know you got em on hold! We got some flamethrowers here! They say they came from Camp Carce!"

The people in the diner all started talking again, and a few yelled welcomes to the kids and teens.

"Well, congratulations, ya'll. What do you need first? You'll need a good meal first thing!" She said, pointing to a large menu behind the bar area but continued, "Or wait," she spotted the injured kid and then noticed all the teens looking worn out and dirty.

She let their silence speak and continued. "I think that some home is needed first. You're safe now. I promise y'all don't need to be adults no more. Follow me."

She led them into the kitchen, which looked like a regular restaurant's kitchen, and the cooks glanced up at the kids, giving them smiles and nods as they walked through it to a large black wall with gold flowers delicately painted on it. She pushed the knife in a knife block, and the wall grew a slit down the middle, becoming a door with a large gold knob that sprouted out of the left side. She walked forward, and out of her finger came a spark that landed on the doorknob, and with that, the doors opened up to show a very large elevator.

"Don't be shy. Come on in and squeeze in. I don't want to be coming back for more of yous. The diner needs their only server. Thems flamethrowers in there are only patient when they gots full coffees."

The kids all held on to each other once they got into the elevator, and it started going down. They had quickly become their only little family, and that feeling passed from one to the other as they held hands, touched shoulders, put arms around each other, as the elevator kept descending. It was such a feeling that Emery herself didn't even fight it. Not even when Jasper reached out and took her hand into his. We both well know that a normal Emery response would have been to push his hand away. But to the surprise of you, I, and Emery herself, she instead squeezed onto it, and it made her feel more powerful than she ever felt before.

11

It All Comes Around

Those foreign elevator doors were now the only thing between these children and the chance at a better life. When they started to open, the chance felt more real than ever, and Jasper's thumb lightly moved across Emery's hand, reminding her to take her first full breath in these long agonizing days.

The doors opened to a massive room where the walls were white, but all painted in different colors, different pictures, and was clearly just a free space for people to be creative. Some of the art drawn directly on the walls looked like true masterpieces by teens or adults, including a brilliant rendition of the famous painting Starry Night. But some of the art drawn on the walls looked as if it was drawn by children, a small house burning, and two stick figures holding hands drawn with what seemed to be finger paints.

In contrast to the free art, eight large chandeliers shined onto the deep wood floors. Emery had never seen anything so brilliant and loved how the chandeliers highlighted the art all around them. Ten or so people were walking around, and a couple of children chased each other. They stepped out of the elevator, stepped forward, and saw a winding bright green staircase right in the middle of the room, in the middle of the art, and in the middle of the flamethrowers playing and working.

"Welcome home." The waitress said, smiling. "I'm Stacy. It's not typically my job to show people around, though. There is a diner to run and like I saids, without coffee this whole place would burn downs." With that, she moved onto the staircase and the students followed. The staircase moved down and they were enclosed again like a cylinder elevator. Emery watched carefully as she shot her hand into the air, and Emery noticed these strange circle openings surrounding them a bit higher in the elevator, all in a different color outline. She shot fire into one of the tubes, and it glowed.

"It's that easy Mill will be done in a moment, and he will show you the ropes. Wait till you meet him." She looked at Dalila, who still held on to Emery.

She bent down to her level, "You really aren't only safe now. You're saved now."

And with that, the staircase moved back up into the room with the art. Stacy waved for everyone to step off the staircase, then she walked through the group and back into the elevator they arrived in. Emery watched her the whole way and analyzed the large black doors she entered. But just then, she felt a tap on her shoulder. The tap felt like it burst her out of a trance, and with that escape from the trance, she also let go of Jasper's hand. It wasn't that she didn't want to hold his hand. But, just like you, what she wants and what she does are often very different things.

"Hey, there, I'm Mill."

"I'm Emery. This is Jasper. These are our friends. We all escaped Camp Carce together. I was told that this would be a safe place for people like us."

Mill had slicked back black hair with bright blue eyes that gave Emery an uneasy feeling. He reminded her of someone, but she couldn't quite place who. She was smart enough to know obviously that she shouldn't judge people based on how they looked. But she was never quite quick enough to overcome the speed at which the judgments came. His voice was raspy and fit his villain-like looks. But the way he talked did not, and his demeanor and smiles gave them comfort even past Emery's first initial judgment.

"Well, you guys sure are lucky. I've never been to the Camp before, but we have a few members here that have been, and we all hear terrible things. I'd say Camp Carce is probably why a lot of us have been staying here so long. It's one of the dangerous things about the outside that it's just hard to overlook. Well, I can say I think you'll like it here much more. Camp Carce is horrendous compared to His Place."

"I'm sorry, what does the his refer to?" Jasper asked, now with his hands crossed and a bit on edge ever since Emery stopped holding his hand.

"You'll get to know him with time." Mill said, putting his hand on Jasper's shoulder. Jasper hated it but didn't move at all as Mill continued, "Our leader came from Camp Carce himself. When he was a young child, his mother told him stories of Camp Carce. She told him he had to go there. That it was the best thing for him. It would be somewhere safe, somewhere he could still exist. When he was at Camp Carce, he realized how wrong those stories really were. After he escaped Camp Carce, he wanted to create something somewhere close to what he had been dreaming of when he was a child. Some place that would make that dream real for other children. So, he created this." He said, pointing around the extravagant room.

"Where does the money come from?" Macy asked quietly as she stepped forward and in between Emery and Jasper, slightly pushing Emery as she did.

Mill smiled and brushed his hair back. He walked towards her. "Mill," he said, putting out his hand and then lighting it aflame a bit. She smiled back and put her hand in his. "Macy." She said, making the flame a bit bigger as she grasped his hand.

"We will start by getting you into some bedrooms. We should have an open wing for just this occasion. Follow me. I'll take you there."

He walked in front, and they got on to the spiral staircase in the middle of the room that the waitress had used to send Mill up. It was more like an escalator the way it moved further and further down as if drilling into the large establishment. It was very dark, with more circles that looked like tubes just outlined in colors surrounding them. It swirled down and made Emery feel a bit unsafe, but she would get used to them with more time.

Mill shot a small flame into a circle that lit up blue, the stairs swirled down a bit more and then stopped, and another large black door appeared and opened. They all followed Mill into a hallway with doors on either side made of what looked to be the same metal from Camp Carce, only here it was painted a brighter blue.

"We have three options for bedrooms currently available. There is the male room, female room, or neutral room where you can find an assortment of feminine and male belongings. You're not stuck with this stuff either. You can order new things at any time; it's just to get you started. Female rooms are labeled with this snowflake." He said, pointing to one of the doors that had an extravagant snowflake carved into it. "Male rooms have the sun." He said, pointing to the other door with a sun with careful details carved into it. "Finally, the neutral rooms have the tree." He pointed to another one that showed a tree with roots that looked like they wrapped around the door.

"Feel free to take whichever rooms you wish." He looked at a fancy black watch on his wrist. "I'll be back in, let's say, one hour. We can grab some snacks and take the rest of the tour." As if those words were the starting whistle of a race. They all started running to different rooms and entering them. Jasper walked calmly past all the kids as they pushed and shoved into different bedrooms. He planned to walk as far as he needed to. He would get the farthest room, so long as everyone else was happy. He didn't care much about where he would lay his head at night.

Emery walked slowly behind him and watched his dark reddish hair bounce as he walked, she also took note of the different rooms each kid was taking. She thought before that once they arrived somewhere safe, her next focus would be solely on the missing kids. After she gets the missing kids here, she could be on her own again. But here they were, and she did not stop feeling like she had to protect this group. There were about 15 more rooms remaining. Some of the kids were checking each other's rooms, and some were just laughing in the hall.

Jasper opened the door to a room to the left with a sun engraved on it. But before he could step inside, he heard the door directly across from him open as well. He turned around and saw the back of Emery's head as she opened the door with the extravagant snowflake and walked into the room. He looked at all the other available rooms and smiled to himself as he entered.

Emery wasn't quite sure what she was expecting from these rooms. But she certainly wasn't expecting what she found. The room was rather big and had a graffiti mural across the largest wall that used orange, yellow, and red and said "Home" A large red bed was in the middle of the room with antique-looking white posts. A white couch sat in front of the bed and faced a large TV that hung over the fireplace. It was the most magnificent bedroom that Emery had ever been in. She walked over to another door on the right wall and opened it up.

A closet that was the size of her bedroom at home was there. It was half-full of clothes and multiple different sizes and colors were available to her. She picked out some blue jeans and a floral top. She just thought she would look pretty in it, and she couldn't deny that after days of fighting, she wanted to look pretty, even if only for a moment.

As soon as she put it on, she looked in a large full-length mirror in the room. She couldn't quite decide if it would make her look pretty or weak in the top. So she took it off and threw it on the ground. She immediately didn't like that she had associated pretty with weak, so she picked it back up. As she held the floral top and looked at herself shirtless in the mirror, she thought about how she didn't even like it and that she shouldn't have to wear flowers to feel pretty anyway. So, she put the blouse back on the rack and vowed she would be brave enough to wear it one day, as a compromise with herself.

She instead picked a plain long-sleeved black top and some black plain converse shoes. She set them on the bed, and as she did, she also took a moment to slide her hand along the comforter. It felt light as air and it was so soft. She already missed her comforting lavender sheets from home, but this would do, this would definitely do. She went to the other door she hadn't opened yet and opened the door to find the bathroom. It wasn't as extravagant as the other parts of the room. But it had everything she needed with a nice shower and silver appliances and handles. She grabbed one of the big, cozy red towels and turned on the shower.

Emery stepped into the shower but didn't make it very long before she was seated in the shower instead. She put her head between her naked knees and let the water run over her like a gentle blanket. She cried a bit. She would never tell you that, and I would never admit I said that to you either.

While Emery cried in the shower, Jasper was across the hall crying in his bed. While they cried in their rooms, Macy cried in the bathroom of the room of the boy she had just made out with, even though she barely knew him at all. Dalila was crying underneath her bed. But most surprising of all, someone Emery knew quite personally was crying in the bedroom directly above hers. Even more surprising than that, someone who owed her the entire world was a couple of floors down, also crying in their shower.

After she cried in the shower for a while, Emery decided that as she stood up, the water would signify peace and strength to her. That each sprinkle, each splash, meant she was closer to the end of all of this. After this moment of strength, Emery left the bathroom and changed into the plain outfit she set out earlier. She crawled into the bed and tightly wrapped the covers over her, so secure she felt like a cocoon. So secure it was as if a love of her life was holding her instead.

She fell asleep quite easily, and just as a dream of her being home in her bed with someone's arms wrapped around her, three quick knocks came to her door, and she jumped up. She grabbed the large key that was on top of the dresser and opened the door to Macy.

"He is going to take us on tour." She pushed her way into the room. "Nice room. It looks pretty similar to mine. But I think we can change them. But also," She said, pausing and looking around, "Ya. Mine is def bigger."

Emery put her hand on Macy's arm and lightly pushed her back out the door. They didn't break eye contact as they both felt the warmth that had developed in the motion. It was too hard to tell if it was from Macy's arm or Emery's hand, but Emery let go as she felt it. They stared at each other a moment longer until Kain walked up, sporting a new red beanie and asked Macy if they had everyone.

Emery turned around, locked her bedroom, and slipped the key into her pocket as she joined everyone else by the stairs again. She wondered quickly if this was the only key to her room and vowed to insure at some point that it was.

"I hope you guys all found the rooms up to your standards. The truth is that we work very hard to keep everyone comfortable and to make everyone really feel at home, feel safe, and feel saved. But the first place I'll be showing you is the place you can go should you have any complaints. Come on guys, join me back on the stairs." Mill said while smoothing down his gelled back hair.

Emery hesitantly joined them on the stairs, and it felt as if they went farther back up to which point, she had to imagine they were close to the artsy room they started in. Mill blasted another small ball of fire into another circle that flashed green, and the stairs moved even further up until they stopped and black doors again appeared. The kids piled into what felt like a large, fancy dentist's office. It had two women in identical blue dresses and one young teen in a blue suit sitting at a desk. "This is The Spark Center!" Mill said as he twirled around, pointing to the people at the desk as they smiled in unison and waved.

"This is where you can order things. You'll come in sometime in the next week and let them know your size, so they can send someone to come collect clothes that don't fit or just aren't to your liking. We will of course, recycle them and make sure another kid somewhere, flamethrower or not, gets good use from them. You'll also be able to start ordering things; maybe you want certain clothes, paintings, pretty much whatever. You come here, and they order it."

"Just whatever we want?" Macy asked.

"You'll each have a personal budget of how much money you can spend. But the guards will let you know that budget when they call to set up your appointment. That's out of my hands. But most people have a pretty large budget." He walked closer to Macy, and for a moment, everyone thought they might actually kiss. "You should see my room sometime. I've got a projector of stars that cover every inch." And before she could respond, he kept walking right back to the stairs. It took Emery completely off guard. Mill looked very young, maybe even her age. But also seemed in a position of authority here and that had really given her the creeps. Another guy that made her realize love just didn't seem worth it sometimes.

"Now, let's go ahead and grab some food. You guys have to be starving."

The next floor they went to when the big black doors opened up from the moving spiral staircase was the most extravagant. In front of the teens was a massive, almost futuristic cafeteria. There was a circle in the middle with tons of food hanging and along the sides there were kitchens putting out hot food of many types, like pizza and cheeseburgers. Most teens were at the tables that were in between the circled walls of food and the kitchens with hot items. It looked like almost 50 teens and Emery couldn't help but feel relieved to see more kids their age.

"I thought you guys ate in the diner?" Jasper asked.

"Sometimes, not very often. The diner is more of a treat for us. You have to get reservations there pretty far ahead of time." Mill pointed to a massive clock in the corner. "Meet you guys back here in 20 minutes, and we will finish out our tour for the day. There will be plenty of time for you guys to explore over the next 50 or so years, anyway." He said, laughing, which left Emery stalling to look at him a moment longer as the other kids stormed the wall full of snacks and grabbed their favorites.

Emery walked over and stood next to Jasper as he looked at a section filled with many different types of Doritos. "You think you'll get Doritos or Doritos?" she said, smiling. He looked at her and smiled, too.

"Emery?"

The voice sent a shiver up Emery's spine. Everything in her froze, and she wanted to hide in Jasper's eyes. She knew that voice. She turned around to find Levi staring right at her. His muscled arms with a deep burn mark scarred into the left one. He had a slight burn going up to his neck as well. But other than that, he looked pretty much the same as always, pretty much as handsome as Emery remembered him.

"Levi."

Jasper stepped forward next to Emery. How could she possibly explain who Levi was to Jasper? This is the boy who broke my heart. This is the boy whose life I ruined. This is the boy who made me never want to fall for another again. The reason there will never be more than that hand holding with

Jasper. This is the boy who started this whole adventure that would ultimately change everyone in the world's lives. This is the boy she lit on fire.

She decided to go simply, "Jasper, this is Levi."

"Levi, what are you doing here?" Emery asked before the two boys could say anything to each other.

"Don't you remember?" touching his scars gently but continuing before Emery could stop him. "You burned me the night of our first date. The ambulance that took me was actually undercover diner members. They saved me, brought me here to live since everything is different now." He said, snapping flames between his fingers.

"Levi, you have to know that I didn't mean to. I didn't know."

Jasper put his hand on Emery's arm. "We should get food. We only have so much time."

"That's ok." Levi continued. "If you hadn't done what you did, I wouldn't be here. I wouldn't know him. I wouldn't know what home felt like."

Jasper's grip around Emery's arm tightened a bit, and for a moment, Emery felt she did know what home felt like, or at least she was beginning to learn.

"I'll let you eat," Levi said, looking at Jasper's hand around Emery's arm. "I'll see you later, and I will truly thank you then." Then he walked away and sat at a table with other teens all chatting.

It was this encounter that unnerved Emery. Something was different about Levi, and she was sure it wasn't just his new power. She also wasn't sure what he meant when he said he would thank her. But she put him on her list. This time it wasn't on her list of people to save, it was of people she had to worry about. She felt guilty for what she did to him. She hadn't even considered she had turned him into one of them. But more than that, she felt scared of what he was now capable of.

Jasper and Emery grabbed all their food and took a seat at an empty table to eat.

"Jasper, I have to leave soon." she said, opening up one of the bags of Doritos.

"I understand." He said, not looking at her. "I think we should leave once we know this is a safe place for every-one else."

"I'm going alone."

"We can do this the easy way or the hard way, Emery. I will break out and follow you from a small distance the whole way, or we can just leave together."

Emery didn't respond, but she knew she would leave without him. She took note to make sure he couldn't know when or how she was planning on leaving. She was beginning to feel some sort of way about Jasper. She couldn't deny it. Even worse, she couldn't deny some child in her screaming for her to fall in love.

But she had other priorities. She had to go save the other children, find the lost children, and do it all without harming anyone else. But the soft part of her hoped when she was all done, she would return. She would find some happiness.

Maybe she would have her first kiss. Maybe she would love it. Even more, maybe she would be able to see her dads occasionally. But she couldn't feel joy until she felt relief.

Once the teens had stopped eating, they noticed Mill arrive from the moving spiral staircase. The kids who had escaped Camp Carce together all gathered back up by Mill, and piled back into the moving spiral staircase.

"Let's see, we have a couple more areas to go to." Mill said while looking at some sort of a map.

Emery's voice rose from the back of the kids, "I would like to meet this leader everyone has been talking about."

Mill's eyes grew a bit big, and he looked like a child who just saw Santa Claus.

"You can meet him one at a time. His presence isn't meant for all of you at once. I'll take you to him while we all check out the Rec Room."

He shot fire into another hole, and the stairs began moving. This time, it was almost too hard to tell if the stairs were going up or down.

12

Not a God

The doors revealed themselves, and Mill motioned for Emery to take a step down and out of the elevator in front of them. Emery stepped off the stairs, and before she moved to the door. She looked back and locked eyes with Jasper. He looked worried but nodded in encouragement, anyway. Then Mill shot another piece of fire, and the kids were gone as the stairs moved.

She turned, and the large black doors closed behind her. It was a white dome room she was in now. Light came through the walls and ceiling and felt almost blinding. There was nothing besides light and white in the room, as far as Emery could tell. Then a large fire seemed to start from nowhere, and Emery stepped back. The fire all of a sudden went down to nothing, and a man stood there instead.

He was tall and handsome. He had dark curls and dark features, but these bright orange eyes that were piercing. He wore all black and a long black coat over it all. He smiled at Emery, and for some reason, she stepped back when he did.

"Don't be afraid." His voice was soft and comforting. He continued. "I'm Elias. It's Emery, correct?"

"Yes."

He smiled again and then spoke to the ceiling.

"Chairs, please."

Two women came from what was seemingly a wall but she wasn't sure how and looked closely for a door. The women carried out two shiny silver chairs and sat them in the room.

"Thanks, ladies." He said, taking a seat and pointing to the other chair as the ladies left. This time Emery observed them and saw them leave through a door barely visible on the side of the dome. She walked around and sat in the chair.

"I want to make sure my friends are safe here. So, I need to know a few things." Emery began talking in a stern voice that showed his comforting looks or voice wouldn't fool her.

"Well, then I have good news, Emery. Not only are your friends safe here. You are safe here."

"Why are you in charge of this place?"

"I was the first."

"The first what?"

"The first flamethrower. I was born with this power. We stay here to grow strong, and to be safe. In exchange, we will do favors sometimes to show our appreciation for the power."

"Ok, slow down. That's a lot to unpack."

"That's the problem, Emery." He stood up, behind his chair and leaned on to it instead. "You don't need to unpack anything. Can I ask? Why do you live like that? Why would you live by taking all these problems on to yourself? Why are you trying to save everyone still? You already saved them. Unpack all this stress, unpack all this pressure you put on yourself, relax and be safe for once."

Emery did not like the way he was now standing as she sat. She mimicked him and stood from her chair and leaned on the back of it. He had a slight smile in the corner of his mouth as she did this.

"Because to not ask questions is a good way to be controlled. No, it's a good way to be manipulated. It's the favorite strategy of many, many terrible people throughout history, as I'm quite sure you know. So, let's start with what concerns me the most, but don't get too comfortable because I've got a lot of questions. What do you mean people who live here sometimes do favors?"

"People who live here know what I mean. It would only be a favor to help us stay safe, to help make this feel like home. It's not your concern right now. Again, you really shouldn't have any concerns right now. You're safe now."

"I don't love how you aren't answering my questions."

He stared at her, seemingly a bit confused. Then she continued, "It doesn't make me feel safe how you aren't really answering any of my questions."

"That's because you haven't caught the flame yet. You don't need questions anymore. You don't need to solve anything. You're home, and I will take care of you."

"Thanks, but I have a dad. Two, in fact. What I need is reassurance that nothing strange will happen to them while I leave."

He laughed deeply. "Now that's a lot to unpack. What do you mean by strange?"

"Will you hurt them?"

"Never." He began to pace the room a bit. "Did I hear

you say leave? Why would you want to leave here? You just arrived."

"I have some things I have to take care of."

"It's not safe in this world for people like us yet. We don't leave my diner until it is safe. I'm working on making the world a safer place for people like us. I've got undercover flamethrowers in the government all over the place. We are working on it. But until there is some real overall change, you are going to need to stay here."

"I plan on returning. But I will be leaving in the morning."

"Unfortunately, I can't allow that. You could put us all at risk, Emery, including your dear, dear friends."

Emery was silent for the first moment since she met Elias. She was deciding how to confront this strange man. His naturally comforting presence somehow gave her a very uncomfortable feeling. She also had a feeling she would need to sneak out of this place, which might take her a bit more time than she was initially expecting. So, what she needed now was more information to help her escape. She had to pick her words carefully. She would not cause a scene, but instead be as quiet as a fox hunting its prey.

"That makes sense." She looked around the dome. "How do you afford all of these nice things for all of these people?"

She was laying her trap, but first, she needed to make him look in the other direction.

"Emery, you're not quite there. But we will get you there. It's not your responsibility anymore to know everything." He moved around and sat back at the chair. "Have a seat again."

Emery walked around and sat with her arms crossed unintentionally as he began speaking again.

"It must be exhausting. All these questions. Do you know where questions come from? A place of fear. You question everything because you're scared. You're questioning everything because you feel like you're responsible. You have to take the whole world on your shoulders. But that's the whole point of here. All of that is finally over. This heavy bag of worries you've been carrying you can finally put down. You have everything here, everything you could ever want. You're home, and you're safe. You know, in most religions, they have some version of here. But the problem is you always have to die first." He leaned in closer to her, "You don't have to die to be at peace, Emery. You just had to come home."

"That all sounds great. I see you have many great resources for us, like the diner. That's really cool. Can I be vulnerable with you?"

He scooted his chair closer to hers. "Always."

"I think I kind of like a boy here."

He smiled, feeling like he had finally broken down the question-loving girl. "I see. Well, that is pretty exciting. Can I ask? Is it Levi? We get to know our family pretty well, and we of course know how he received his powers, Emery."

She frowned; the mention of Levi had totally thrown her off her game. She had to focus again on the plan that she was building as word by word it was falling out of her mouth.

"Levi is very sweet. But it's not Levi. It's a boy I came with, that's what I need your help with Elias."

He leaned back in his chair and put his hand through his curls, then smiled, "I see. I would be happy to help you, Emery. What can I do for you?"

"I've never been on a date before."

"Well, that's not completely true now, is it Emery?"

She looked up at him with burning eyes that almost blew her vulnerable cover, but she fixed them quickly, "Well yes, but Levi and I never really went on that date. As I'm sure you well know, it seems."

"I'd love to talk more about Levi. One of the great programs we offer here is counseling. I know that how you obtained this power and how you have accidentally passed it are both very traumatizing events. I will have you set up for a session tomorrow. But anyway, this boy. Who is it?"

"His name is Jasper."

"I see." He said, scooting a bit closer and putting his hand on her shoulder. "I have seen that you guys seem rather close, or so I've been told. So, is it that you want a date with this boy?"

"Yes, I was hoping maybe we could eat dinner in the diner?"

"Well, usually, it's pretty hard to get a reservation there. But I think we could work something out. How about tomorrow evening?"

"That would be perfect. I would really appreciate it."

"I think I could make that happen. See Emery, all you need to do is trust me. All your other responsibilities are gone now. You're finally at peace."

"I'm starting to see that."

"Do you need anything else right now?"

"No, I think that's it. How would I contact you if I do?"

"You can always go to the secretary floor and ask for me, and we can set up an appointment because I am always here for you."

"Thanks."

"Has Mill taught you how to use the stairs?"

"Not really."

"It's pretty easy and quite fun—a good way to practice those powers safely. I won't ever make you hide your powers. Here they are a gift, and you can use them with the confidence that they will be safe. "

He pulled a small ipad out of his coat and started typing on it.

"Great, it looks like your friends are all hanging out in the rec room for the evening. I'll teach you how to get there. Follow me."

He said, getting up and walking to the doors, but never taking his eyes off Emery.

She followed him on the spiral stairs and felt uncomfortable as the doors closed, and it was just the two of them on the spiral staircase. He pointed out the many-colored holes that appeared after the door closed that she had already noticed.

"Do you see those little holes?"

"Yes." She said, annoyed with his mannerisms that made her feel stupid.

"You just shoot a flame into them to go to a certain floor. You see those holes at the bottom." She had not noticed more colored circles underneath. "Those are the different wings of the building, so you can go to another wing first."

"It's almost magical."

"Almost being the keyword. It's just some brilliant tech some of our brilliant pyro engineers created. Here."

He handed her a rolled-up piece of paper. Emery's first thought was how it could be a weapon. It would help her fire grow.

"That's a map of the different wings and floors."

She opened it to see the outline of the elevator and the floors available. He leaned over her shoulder. "We are already in the green wing. So, we don't need to change wings, but what one do we need to activate to go to the rec floor?"

She looked over the map, and before asking or responding to him, she looked up and found the orange circle in the darkness. She put her hand up and tried to make a small flame shoot through the hole. Instead, as if all the fake vulnerability she had portrayed had bundled her courage up inside of her into a ball, a massive ball of flame shot out and covered a mass area of the holes. Emery quickly looked to Elias.

Elias's warm and welcoming face dropped. He looked angry, and she saw his eye twitch slightly as he looked in the direction the flame went in. He shook his head, and the anger fell off it, and he smiled.

"Well, Emery. That's fascinating. I would like to do some work with you. We need to control that. Can you try one more time?"

She took a deep breath and closed her eyes. A small flame. A small flame. A small flame. And with that, a small flame shot out, and she quickly pointed it to the orange hole. The staircase began to move, and they stood in silence until it stopped and the doors were revealed.

She stepped off the stairs, and she was surprised when he did, too. She was even more surprised as the door started opening that he stood directly behind her and put his hands on her shoulders like she was his child. Then walked into the rec room with her.

The rec room had games all around in a large room with wooden beams standing between them. There was ping pong, arcade games, pool, and so much more. Kids were laughing and playing at all of the games. She noticed off to the side were more rooms with couches, bars, and TVs where adults were laughing and talking just as much. But everyone stopped when Emery and Elias entered. Emery didn't know why a bunch of kids came running over and gasping at Elias as if he was a celebrity.

"Elias, can you touch my hand?" A young girl with brown pigtails asked. He smiled and kissed the outside of her hand.

Another little boy with brown spikey hair came up.

"Elias, I just won at ping pong." Elias stepped around Emery and knelt near the boy. "I'm proud of you." He said as he put his hand firmly on his shoulder. Then he stood up and looked at all the kids.

"I must be on my way, children. I love you." With that, the children all responded with, "We love you." Back to Elias. It was that moment. It was the synchronized we love you that shifted Emery's focus quickly and made her realize that Elias was very wrong earlier. Emery was not free, she was not home, and they certainly weren't safe. Everyone here seemed to treat this man as if he was a god, and she could think of nothing more dangerous than a false god.

She mentally adjusted her list.

Escape

Free the other children from Camp Carce

Find the lost children

Return and free these children and adults at the diner

Find somewhere actually safe for everyone

She felt comfortable leaving the children and adults for now. She knew that Camp Carce was obviously dangerous and a bad environment. The diner, in her opinion, was just as dangerous. But to the people here, it felt safe. She would let them live in ignorance while she went to free the others from Camp Carce. Then she would burn them all down, both Camp Carce and His Place Diner itself.

After Elias left, the kids all went back to playing, and Emery looked for anyone familiar. She thought she just wanted to look for people she knew to see if they were doing ok. But that wasn't the truth, if we are honest. We all know who she was actually looking for. She spotted Macy, Jose, and Kain playing ping pong. But she kept looking. Then she walked over to the foosball table, where she saw Jasper playing with a girl she didn't recognize.

The girl playing with him was unconventionally pretty. Emery liked this about her. She didn't wear any makeup and had very sharp features that felt powerful. She wasn't jealous, but she liked her immediately. Funny how you always know who is good or bad right when you meet them. It's this part of you that screams when you see them. Humans have just become very good at stifling that scream, just like they stifle everything else.

"Hey, I'm Emery." She said with a smile to the girl.

"Kella," she said as she flipped her foosball players to score a winning goal.

"How'd it go?" Jasper asked.

"It went fine. Kella, how long have you been here?"

"Three years as of yesterday. It was my home party yesterday. I wish you guys had been there. It was seriously off the wall fun." She said, now looking away from the game she won.

"What's that?"

"They throw you a celebration on the anniversary of when you first came here. It's kind of like our birthdays."

"And what about your birthdays?" Jasper asked as he recounted the goals, trying to focus on the conversation and not that he had lost, fighting his bad habit of turning games into unfun battles.

"Just home parties."

"That's kind of weird." He said, a little bit bitter from the game.

Kella looked up from the table at Jasper and gave a gentle shh and pointed at a camera. Jasper looked at the camera and then at Emery, who just nodded at him, reassuring him she had more to share with him later.

"It's great." Kella continued. "It was a great party. You guys will have to wait a year, but we will have so much fun. I swear. They are like my favorite days here, honestly."

"Kella, are you happy here?" Emery asked, knowing she

might not get a real answer, remembering the camera Kella had pointed out. But sometimes humans ask questions, not because they expect the truth. But because there is always some sort of truth hidden in any answer. You just have to look in the right place.

"We are all happy here." This answer told Emery a few things. Whatever these kids were feeling it certainly was not happy. The collective "we" and "home" and "safe"were being used to pull their strings. Emery knew she had a pretty hard challenge ahead of her when it came to taking this place down. That was enough information for now though, she didn't want to push Kella anymore than she already had. But she got lucky when Kella looked up to her, and Emery spotted tears imprisoned in her eyes. This gave her more answers.

"I think I'm going to go to my room for a while before dinner. I think I need some time to rest before more of these fun activities. I'm sure you understand." Emery said, then looked to Jasper as if sending a hint. This was a strange moment for our dear Jasper. He felt completely breathless. Here Emery had been playing as if she wasn't interested this whole time, and now, out of nowhere, she wanted him to go to her room. He was flattered. He quickly resolved he needed to decide whether this was what he wanted to do. He was too busy being excited that she was interested in him, that he hadn't yet resolved his own interest. Examining his own interest in spending time with Emery alone took approximately five seconds, and if I'm being honest, that was three seconds longer than I was expecting from him.

"I was just about to head to the rooms, too. I think I'll take a shower and get a nap in. I'll go with you Emery." He said, letting go of his foosball abruptly and almost forcefully. Even Kella herself smiled at this.

"See ya, Kella. It was nice to meet you. Really, I hope we see each other again."

With that, Emery and Jasper walked off together. Macy watched them as they walked out the doors, and she took note. She was developing a new plan herself; she would ruin Emery. She decided she wanted Jasper, and she knew exactly what was in her way. At that moment, she made plans to drown the fire that was inside that girl.

They entered the stairs, and the door closed. Emery showed Jasper the map that Elias had given her and pointed to the wings.

"So, the rooms are in the blue wing and he labeled my room for me here. So blue she pointed towards the lower chutes, and red she pointed to the higher ones. Go ahead and try."

Jasper quickly released a fireball into both, and the stairs started moving. Only now, as they stood on the rotating stair-case, did the silence of the stairs make its presence known. Emery was not particularly scared of her quite scary plans. She wasn't scared of Camp Carce or Elias. But whatever was laying in this silence. Whatever was breathing down their necks every time, these two were alone together. That was the single scariest thing she had ever encountered.

13

An Escape for Two

When the stair ride finally stopped and Emery and Jasper got off the winding stairs to start walking down the hallway, Emery finally fully took a breath. She whispered to him as they walked,

"My room."

He was losing all the confidence he naturally had from being handsome for many years.

"Ok." He said in a shaky voice.

When they got to her bedroom, she took her key out and slowly opened the door. It made her uncomfortable to find strawberries out and a fire going. She started looking for cameras in the room. On the other hand, Jasper took a seat in front of the fire and had a couple of strawberries as he watched her inspect every corner for cameras. To her relief, she didn't see any. The staging with strawberries and the fire must have resulted from them watching them in the rec room, maybe the stairs and the hallway. Maybe since the moment they had first stepped foot in His Place Diner. She was relieved to not find any cameras in her room, though, and she sat down next to Jasper.

Jasper put his hand through his hair and wished desperately that he had showered today.

"Thanks for coming." She said, grabbing a strawberry. "I wanted to talk to you about a date tomorrow."

Our poor dear Jasper slumped a bit as she said this. He thought this was a date, heck he even thought it could be more than a date. But then he sat up a bit straighter as he considered the possibilities. He would take a date tomorrow, happily, because with each moment he was resolving more and more, he would take any time with her that he could find.

"Not a real date. But I need to escape, and it was the only way I could think to get us in the diner."

Poor Jasper slumped right back down and took another strawberry. This time, he bit it angrily as he looked at the fire. He threw a fireball into the fire to make it light up even larger.

"Two things," He said, staring blankly at the fire.

"What?"

"It's a real date." He smirked and looked at her. "Number two, I'm going with you."

"On the date? Yes, of course. I need you there honestly."

"No Emery. I'm going with you back to Camp Carce."

"Jasper, it's too dangerous."

"For who?"

"You."

"But not for you?"

"Jasper, I'd rather you didn't." She said, looking at him sweetly, and there was something Jasper didn't like about it. He wanted Emery and didn't like that she was only giving that energy back in order to get him not to do something. He quickly switched from flirty to assertive.

"I'll be clear with you, Emery. Either I go with you, or I go talk to that weird leader guy about your plan before you can go through with it."

"You wouldn't."

"You know how you're trying to do everything to get me to stay? I promise you I'll do more to make sure you're safe, and if I can't go with you, my best option is to keep you here."

Any romance, any light flirting, was officially out the window. Their stubborn selves stared into each other, and challenge was in the air. Emery gave it a moment, then decided it wasn't worth the risk. Although he was willing to risk the lives of the lost children and the children at Camp Carce to save her, she was not willing to risk any of them to save him, no matter how she felt about him.

"Ok, we leave tomorrow evening." This surrender allowed for more sweet surrenders.

"After our date, though?"

Emery smiled for the first time since they entered the room.

"After dinner, before dessert."

"I'll take that. Emery, I know how they get the stuff here. Kella told me the secretary's name is Asa, and she has a car. She said it's parked out back, and the keys are in her desk."

Emery laughed, "Why would you have that information?"

"I knew you'd be planning already. Seems like you never really rest, so I got to thinking about how the others leave. I figured another backpacking trip. Although, romantic sure."

He said, scooting a bit closer to her, "Would actually be terrible and maybe a nice drive would be preferable."

They spent the rest of the evening detailing their plan to escape, their plan to get back to Camp Carce, and their plan once they got there. They ended up sitting on the floor next to the fire as they planned out each step. They didn't have any paper, so together, they created an acronym to help them remember.

Plan Flamingo

F- fires to get them out of the diner

L- leave his awful and dangerous diner

A-Asa's car and drive towards camp carce (west)

M-Make it to Camp Carce, park the car

I-Impersonate keepers to get inside

N-Navigate the areas, find the main security, and unlock all doors

G-Get everyone together at the Estrella's cabin

O-organize for them all to come here once they were safe at the cabin. That way they can come to the diner to help save the rest of the flamethrowers.

Emery decided not to share with Jasper that this was only half her plan. Her next plan was to find an actual safe place for flamethrowers. She knew that something was off here as well, but it was better than Camp Carce. Even though Jasper had placed himself in this situation, she was hoping she could handle the other issues on her own. Their plan wasn't very detailed, and they knew that. But part of the plan was trusting in themselves and what they were capable of, just like her dad's original plan for her. Both of them realized that sometimes the best strategy was just faith.

They were also just assuming that the lost children were at Camp Carce. It was the only place they could imagine they had ended up. They weren't sure where they would end up next. They talked, they planned, and they envisioned the worst. Until Emery fell asleep in Jasper's lap, this was the real moment. This was the moment Jasper realized he did not just like Emery. There was something so vulnerable about her at that moment. She was talking just before, but blinking heavily.

"When we take the small children to the second cabin...on the way here..." Then she laid on his lap. He held his breath as she continued speaking.

"We should make holders, like little baby carriers. That way, we can carr..." She fell asleep then, mid-sentence and mid-thought. There was something so sweet and gentle about this strong girl that he couldn't help but sit there and look at her sleeping. For as long as he could before, he felt too tired and too creepy to continue. So, he laid his head back and slept with his legs crossed just so that he wouldn't wake Emery up.

When she woke in the morning, she woke up with a sort of panic. She had not intended to sleep cuddled up next to Jasper by the fire. She quickly got up and physically rubbed at herself like her vulnerability with him could be seen still on her clothes. When she moved, he woke up too. He slowly got up and moved his legs physically with his hands as they were frozen in the uncomfortable position he had fallen asleep in.

Emery felt very bad at that moment, at first thinking he

was disgusted by her but quickly realizing he hadn't moved all night just to keep her comfortable. There was a knock on the door, and they both jumped a bit.

Emery held out her hand to Jasper and helped him stand, then motioned for him to stay as she went to open the door. Two coffees sat on a tray outside the room. She walked out to get them and saw Macy staring at her from down the hall. She raised her eyebrows at Emery, and something in Emery burned, but she held it in, grabbed the coffees, and closed her door. She set the coffees on the bed. Jasper grabbed one of them, "Creepy." He said as he started walking away.

"Wait," Emery said, and he turned.

"Wait till, after coffee, Macy is out there being weird. She is probably just waiting for you to walk out the door so she can start all sorts of rumors."

"Emery, I'll wait as long as you want me to."

They sat down and had their coffees in silence as they both woke up and realized that despite their sweet moments; they had a large evening and the next couple of days ahead of them. As Jasper started to finish, "I'll get Asa's keys."

"Try not to get them too early, or she will notice. How are you going to get them?"

"Believe it or not, Ms. Emery, not everyone is as good as you at avoiding my charms."

"Unfortunate souls." She said, but she looked up from her coffee sweetly.

"We need outfits for the Keeper impersonations. I'm going to try to get a bunch of clothes from her and steal the keys at the same time. I'll make sure I get all sorts of colors and

I'll wear only the black ones to our date and underneath my outfit. You," he smiled, "Can wear whatever you want to our date of course."

"I think I'll probably just wear clothes that will be comfortable to travel in."

He nodded at her seriously, then she continued.

"Or maybe I'll wear a nice dress." She said, sipping from her coffee again.

"Well, maybe I'm really looking forward to it. I'll see you later Emery. I'm going to get started. I could not give less of a shit if Macy is still out there or not." He said, putting his coffee down on the table and leaving the room. It wasn't until he actually left that Emery began feeling bad. Some hidden part of her thought he would kiss her.

Then she worried she was ruining any possible chance she had with him. But she could not reason pursuing this attraction, pursuing anything like this with the pressure of saving so many children resting in her mind. This was what she told herself, at least. But she was also quite scared of what happened with her first crush. Could she even fall in love with someone? Or was she bound to burn them if she did?

Unlike Jasper, Emery stayed in her room for the rest of the day, only leaving for food, and even when she did that, she made sure to avoid others as she grabbed it and returned to her bedroom. She was notified via a note under her door that her reservation for His Place Diner was at 5 pm.

She started getting ready at three, and she had some serious decisions to make. She wanted to dress nicely to look nice for a date. But, she also knew that what she wore would determine what she would wear to make the journey back to Camp Carce and to fight against her original kidnappers. She went with some jeans and a hoodie, looking for comfort. But immediately felt like she should wear the dress she hinted at. She pulled a beautiful red dress from her closet and tried it on. It fit her perfectly and showed a woman that she wasn't quite ready to reveal. She looked beautiful. Then she wondered if she would look this beautiful when the waitress Stacy traps her in a prison for trying to escape but not being able to move fast enough in a skin-tight red dress. So, she took the dress off quickly, as if it was falling apart in the moment, and put back on her jeans and hoodie.

But she had another plan to impress Jasper that did seem less dangerous. She did her makeup and based it on youtube videos she had watched for days on end for her first date. She wasn't quite sure if she would regret her decision to wear the makeup. She pictured what she might look like with day-old makeup after they had slept in the car for a night. But she couldn't resist the opportunity to feel pretty. She wanted to have that moment more than she was scared of the aftermath of her makeup application.

She finished with ten minutes to spare and laid on her bed, thinking about what the rest of her life would look like. She allowed herself to be selfish for a moment, to think of herself for only these ten minutes. After that, she would continue to focus on saving others. But the ten minutes was only five minutes of selfishness before there was a knock on her door. She opened the door to find Jasper looking more handsome than she had hoped. He also went casual with his clothes, for the same reasons as Emery. But, he spent more time on his hair and had a freshly shaved face, and looked quite handsome.

"You ready?" He said, opening his arm for her to take it. She took his arm, even though it made her a bit uncomfortable. But she knew she had to keep the facade going because, obviously, they were being watched. As she was pulled in closer, she smelled a strong cologne on him she never noticed before. It was so strong it made her want to cough and yet also made her want to bathe in his scent herself. They headed down the hallway quietly. A couple of the kids and teens were in the hall and giggled and whispered as the couple made their way down that hallway that never seemed longer than it was in this very moment, and to the staircase.

When the doors to the staircase closed and they were again in the dark, she instinctively held on a bit harder to Jasper's arm, and he felt content in her squeeze for safety. But this made him wonder exactly how safe he could actually keep this brave girl. Jasper flew his flame into the green space, and the staircase moved. She squeezed a bit harder as she moved in closer to him, he even thought, for just a moment, that he could feel her shaking.

The doors opened, and they found themselves in the full diner. Stacy, the waitress with the heavy accent and loud shoes, greeted them with a huge smile at the opening doors.

"Right on time. I have a reservation for Jasper and Emery?"

"That's right," Jasper said, nudging Emery a bit.

The woman led the two teens to a booth in the corner of the diner. As she walked, Emery noticed she had a slight limp and saw blood dripping out of her shoe upon looking a little closer. She noted this woman as someone else she would try to save one day, and she realized that her list of people to save was getting longer every day, and therefore her life and living for her own adventure grew shorter every day.

They snuggled into the booth, and Jasper was slightly touching her body in it.

"Drinks?" The woman asked with a dead tone.

"Water," Emery answered.

"Beer," Jasper answered.

To both of their surprise, she didn't respond and just walked away to get started. Jasper smiled at Emery.

"I just thought it was worth a shot." He said, chuckling a bit, "Didn't think I'd actually get one."

Emery smiled just a bit. It was just enough for him to feel as if he had a blanket from her cold, but not enough that he felt warm.

"So, what's the plan?" Jasper offered the question as more of a relief from his biggest fear, awkward silences, than from genuine intrigue.

She laughed at the uncomfortable question considering they spent all night planning. "After we eat, we walk out like we are leaving. But I'll start a fire, and we will make a run for the door."

"You think the fire is necessary?"

She looked around at the people in His Place Diner with suspicion.

"Yes, I do. Something is very wrong here, and I imagine it's not as easy as it looks to leave. "

"Then why are we going back to Camp Carce if this place is just as bad?"

The woman returned and set the water and beer down.

"Have ya'll had any chances to read the menu?"

"Not yet," Jasper answered. "We are just enjoying each other's company." He said, putting his arm around Emery's shoulder. Instinctively Emery looked at it, unsure but quickly smiled, looking back at the woman.

"Alright, just give me a shout when you ready." They watched as she walked away. Jasper removed his arm from around Emery.

"Sorry, I should have asked. I was just trying to keep appearances up."

"I didn't mind it," Emery responded, looking down at the menu. She wasn't planning on telling Jasper about her theories about the diner. But she was sure he was already figuring it out and if they were going to be working together, she thought her best choice was to start telling him the truth, if anything, for his own safety. He was getting a little too comfortable here just like all the other teens and kids they brought with them, just like all the other flamethrowers that were in the diner around them.

Her eyes moved up from the menu as she continued talking. "This place is a secret evil, hidden behind a curtain. Camp Carce isn't even trying to hide it. That's why I think it takes priority now. I could be wrong, but we can only make choices based on what we know. Not to mention I can only do one thing at a time, and the missing children are my biggest priority."

Jasper took a moment to look at the menu as he spoke, "Well, I'm with you 100%, But I also can't just leave behind the kids here if you think they are in danger."

"You could stay, Jasper." She said, feeling like she had just fit the final puzzle piece in, only to discover it definitely did not fit.

"That's not what I'm saying, Emery. I understand that your priority is Camp Carce. But once we save the kids from Camp Carce, we can't just leave the other kids here if you think that something sinister might be happening here."

"I'm not planning on it."

They heard the heels with the limp of Stacy coming up to their side so quickly that Jasper said, "And honestly, that's why Kurt Cobain would absolutely despise how long his legacy had gone on for."

"What can I get for ya'll?" Stacy asked, interrupting.

Jasper quickly ordered the steak; a move Emery rolled her eyes at because it would prolong the dinner. Emery ordered a mac and cheese then looked at Jasper afterwards.

"Really? A steak?"

"Look, I'm going to kick some ass soon and I'm for sure going to need some protein for that ass kicking. I can't kick ass on a Caesar salad."

"I think we should probably focus on the rooms when we get to Camp Carce." Emery said, ignoring his protein excuse.

"We have plenty of time to talk about our plan once we get out of here. So, my concern now is that part of this deal involved this being a real date, and I want to know more about you. Are you close to your family?"

Emery's mind had shifted since her adventure began. For her, it was in an instant. The instant she was kidnapped, and she found that she was not alone, she became her true self. She had stepped aside from the scared teen and had quickly forgotten that part of her even existed. She was lucky, in a way. Most people spend their whole lives trying to find who they are. But she had been forced into it.

She was forced into adulthood that she was born for. But there was something about Jasper that continued to remind her that she was still just a teen girl who was actually quite scared of boys.

"I am very close with my family. I live with my two dads, and they really are my everything. They are my why. You know?"

"Ya, I know that feeling. I had it once with my mother before she found out I was a flamethrower."

"What happened?"

"She wasn't too happy about my ability. I was burned in a fire at her work, actually. Kind of ironic it was her fault. She couldn't get me a babysitter and would always bring me with her to the office. One day the police all came swarming the place for some guy they were after, then before we knew it we were in a terrible fire. She got me out, but I still got burned." He showed Emery a burn mark on his wrist as Stacy walked up and set down the beer and water. She smiled, "The mark. You know some have it better than others." She said as she rolled down her stocking to reveal an entirely burned right leg.

Emery and Jasper stared speechless, and Stacy laughed, "Aw don't y'all worry bout ol' me. It's the best thing that ever happened to me." She said as she rolled her stocking back up and walked away to talk to another table.

Emery shook off the choke of Stacy's bluntness, "Your mom though, what happened?"

"Nothing for a while. I went a good year there without any indication that anything was wrong. Then we were at my birthday party, and she put in front of me this massive, beautiful birthday cake. Prettiest one I ever saw. But then the whole family realized no one had a lighter. They were all getting frustrated looking everywhere and all I could think was we just need a little fire." He took a sip of the beer. "I lit the whole table on fire and my mom saw it all. I was scared. I was so scared. I didn't know what it meant, and I needed my mom, you know." He took another sip of the beer. "She said I was a demon brought from the devil to tempt her into hell."

"I'm sorry."

"It's ok. I needed it. Life was a little too good, you know. I had just started to do well at school, big soccer scholarship, homecoming king. Everything good, everything boring, it would have led to me being a boring and probably not even a good person, you know? You need these things to happen. Bad things only happen to the best people." He went in for another sip of the beer, only to realize the three sips were probably just enough. He asked Stacy for water as well as she dropped off their food.

They thanked Stacy for the gorgeous dishes. It was only as they both looked down at the steaming meals that they realized how appreciative they really were. Jasper began cutting into his steak. He said, "Oh man, I think I needed this."

Emery was cutting into hers as well, "Me too. We sure could use it."

Jasper took his first bite, and the pleasure spread to his eyes as he spoke.

"I'm grateful. I can't remember the last time I had a meal like this. But whenever I have these moments, I always think to myself, when's the next time I'll have a meal like this."

"Well, that makes it feel sad."

"Not really. It doubles the gratefulness. If this is my last steak ever, it makes it even sweeter and even juicier. There is no telling when moments are our last. We have to treat them as if they all are."

Emery contemplated this as she ate her own steak and couldn't help but notice it did seem to make it taste better. She thought about this date in this way. Who knew the next time she would have another date? It made her smile in the moment, and she tried to take it in a bit more. She even scooted just a bit closer to him, and she put her hand on his knee. But just for a moment before, she got too scared and took it away. But that moment, no matter which short, meant a whole lot to both of them.

As they finished eating, they both knew that their time was ending. Their date was ending, which meant that their next adventure was coming. The word adventure is quite funny, isn't it? It can describe joy, but it can also describe terror, and in this case, I regret to inform you; it was terror.

"It's almost here. We will get the check and go for it." Emery said, now in a whisper.

"One of the cars is marked, and I got it out of her. She was actually chattier than I expected. It has a green star. Look for the green star, and I'll drive."

Although Emery felt tempted to challenge his driving, she herself had never even gotten her driver's license, yet there was something so tempting in her that she wanted to be in charge of this as well.

The waitress cleared their plates, and the air felt heavier than usual.

"Feel free to stay as long as you like, honeys. Give me a shout if you need anything else." Stacy said.

"Thank you." They said in unison.

"Are you ready?" Jasper asked, rubbing his sweaty palms on his pants.

"Let's give her a minute to get busy again. Hug me. I want to get a better look at the people closest to the door."

"Will you stop needing excuses to be close to me?" he smiled as he pulled her in quickly and more seductive than she had imagined. She almost forgot to look at the people by the door.

She had never been touched by a guy like this before, and it made her stall before she remembered her goal. She saw the closest two booths to the door seemed somewhat safe. One had a family in it with a mother, father, and two little girls. She doubted they were secret security. The other booth has two other teens on a date, and they were too busy kissing currently to notice anything. She pulled back from Jasper.

"A family and a couple. I'm not too concerned. But we have to be fast, and I have to be careful with my fire. I don't want to hurt anyone accidentally."

"I think we should start training."

Emery looked around the restaurant, noting everyone she saw.

"I just don't want to use this power all the time. It's dangerous. Training would just be promoting it."

"But that's not quite true. You are using it, and you have been using it. So, you might as well train, that way you can control it enough not to hurt people."

She looked back at him. "I can see that. We can explore it more over our trip. But now we have to focus." She took a deep breath. "Are you ready?"

"Yes." Jasper said, wiping his hands again on his pants.

When they got up, he pulled her in close and placed her to the side of the door. He put his hand around her waist to ensure she was closest to the exit. Every step they made towards the front door time seemed to move slower and faster all at the same time. The family in the booth near the door glanced up at them as they walked by, probably curious as to why the two teens were not headed back to the elevator that would lead them back to the staircase. Emery looked at the child in the booth. She mouthed, "Run." to the little boy. But he didn't move at all.

They stopped in front of the door, and Emery threw her hand out and a line of powerful fire formed. Jasper pushed the door, but it wasn't moving, so he started to slam into it with his body. People in the diner started yelling and running to the elevator area. The waitress stood on the other side of the fire and stared at the couple, meeting Emery's eyes through the flames.

Jasper pulled the steak knife from dinner out of his pocket that Emery didn't know he had grabbed. He used it to break the glass and pull the door open from the outside. He reached back and grabbed her wrist, tearing her eyes away from the waitress. They made their way through the door and found Elias directly in front of them, holding Macy by the neck.

14

Putting Fires Out

Jasper and Emery stood in front of His Place Diner. Elias and Macy seemed almost frozen in place right in front of them. Emery's left hand was intertwined with Jaspers. She wasn't even sure when they had grabbed eachother's hands. Her other hand was sprayed out, hanging out her side but ready to shoot. She was already thinking about how she could light his fancy feet on fire in a moment. It would make him let go of Macy and give them enough time to run for the car.

"I must admit I'm so disappointed." Elias said with his hand glowing red against Macy's neck.

"I'm sorry." Emery said, "Let her go and we can end this now."

"Oh, I think you are misunderstanding. I don't have her here to bargain with you." He looked at Macy and pulled a piece of hair back to behind her ear. "I have her here because I need her. I know you have some power in you Emery."

Then as he said this, fire began on his hand and he pushed it hard into Macy's neck and it grew massive until she was completely up in flames. She dropped down part ash and part charred pieces of a body. Jasper pulled Emery back as she tried to run towards Macy, not quite believing what she just watched. Not quite ever believing that he had burned Macy to death in front of them. But Elias flew a massive fire ball at them that neither of them had seen before. He yelled at the couple as they ran for the car and dodged the massive fire balls he threw. "You see Emery. I discovered something!" He yelled, beginning to shoot the fireballs at their feet. "I wasn't quite born with this power, just like you! We aren't so different after all. I found that if you completely burn someone you gain their powers for a short time. I knew how helpful this would be!" He said with massive flames starting to cover his entire body.

They got to the car and Jasper and Emery jumped in as a fireball burned part of the back of the car. Jasper quickly pulled out, but now Elias had blocked their exit with a wall of fire larger than the ones Emery had built so far. He reversed into the corner of it, then quickly flipped the car to the side so that Emery was facing him and she quickly began shooting fire back at Elias's fire balls. As the two balls of fire would collide, a small explosion occurred that caught Elias by surprise and gave Jasper and Emery the time to drive away.

Emery looked back, seeing Elias angrily pointing at the teens that were in His Place Diner earlier on their own date to follow Jasper and Emery. Emery saw the waitress sweeping up the ash remains of Macy and putting the left-over body parts in a large trash bag. She was suddenly conflicted between staying and destroying this man or going to Camp Carce now. She had now seen that he was murdering people; they didn't know if that's what was happening at Camp Carce yet.

But it was too late, and she thought again about the missing children and even Phillip, who she worried would have been greatly punished if he returned to Camp Carce as she thought they had.

The two teens they saw making out earlier at the diner were now in a car racing towards Jasper and Emery as they made their way down a dirt road. Emery pulled open the roof window and stood out of it. They began shooting fire at the car and she ducked for a minute.

"Shit," Jasper said as he started weaving to miss the shots.

"I've got em." Emery said as she popped back out from the roof. She shot her hands out and burned both the front tires of the jeep the teens were in. It was her most focused and pointed shot she had made with her fire. The tires melted down to nothing in a moment, and the car flipped forward and landed on the hood. She sat back down, put on her seat belt and leaned over to pull on Jasper's for him as he drove.

They drove the first thirty minutes in complete silence. Emery watching carefully behind her to see if they had any visitors. Jasper making focused and deliberate moves to make sure they had escaped and were finding a more public road to be on before heading in the direction of Camp Carce.

After, 30 minutes they finally stopped, feeling the car rattle as they made their way onto a paved road. As if they both had been waiting for some sort of sign, they were safe; the change in the road brought a breath of relief to each of them.

"I mean we have to go back, right?" Jasper questioned, looking over briefly at Emery for the first time since the escape.

"I've been thinking about it a lot. I still think we hit Camp

Carce first. Especially because of how we just left, we might need help when we go back. The older kids from Camp Carce could help us to save the kids at the diner. Plus, I still think there is something to the fact that they are happy in their ignorance for the moment. Don't get me wrong, we will go straight back to save them."

"I can't believe he killed Macy."

"He seemed like he had done that many times before."

"I didn't know we could be burned." He said quickly, wiping a tear that landed on his cheek.

"He completely burned her, brought her to mostly ashes. I don't think even flamethrowers can live through that. Did you hear what he was saying?"

"I did."

"That must be what that place really is. He burns them when he needs them."

"I knew something was wrong." Jasper said. "I mean, not as much as you. But it didn't feel right. I knew you were right about that. I didn't think it was that bad though." He shook his head, ashamed of himself for not noticing more, for not asking more.

They drove for another hour before Jasper went back onto the dirt roads into the woods, where he found remnants of a former camping site. He parked the car, and they both got out. Emery said as she jumped out of the car, "I'm going to go find wood for a fire." She walked away quickly before he could see her or say anything. She kept walking through the woods and looking back until she found a spot. He couldn't see her.

She then bent down and just started crying. Everything

she had feared since this adventure began came out. Every moment she had seen people hurt or leave came flowing out. All the fear that had been building rushed through the tears. Each tear held a new anxiety, and she felt relief as she let them melt through her without any control.

Jasper was sitting by the tire of the car doing the same thing, only a bit different. He picked at his arm and pinched it and tore at it a bit as he thought about all his fears. He felt tears going, but pushed them down into his throat. A bad habit he had been taught as a child and wouldn't drop until someone finally tore it out of him much later.

They both desperately needed that moment. After a couple minutes, Emery wiped away her tears. She rubbed her eyes roughly and deeply and took a deep breath. She felt so much better and as she stood up. She looked up to the sky. She spoke to those who had left before her, which now included Macy. "I'll never stop, I promise."

She started to head back to the spot, but then quickly realized she didn't grab any wood. Jasper watched as she picked up a few pieces of wood and sticks close to the camp spot. He got up off the ground and brushed himself off, then ran towards her to take some from her hands and throw into the fire pit that had been left by previous campers.

They both sat near it as Jasper shot a fire out in the fire pit. They had a lot to discuss, but the words had kind of escaped them both. It was the silence that felt like power in the moment. Jasper walked up and sat next to Emery. He put his arm around her. This time it wasn't so she could look out for something, or so he could protect her. It was something different. She melted into it and cuddled up against him. She hadn't known how much she really need that moment as well.

They made a plan for the day tomorrow, which mostly consisted of violent flames. I noticed, even though they didn't, that something about both of them had been rougher since Macy's murder. The plan was to burn what they needed and take it by what came. Neither had a good idea of the structure of the building, so they would have to just hope they were enough and that they could outsmart them somehow.

They made their way back into the car at night and pulled back the front chairs to laying down and at first, they faced each other.

"I have to tell you something, Emery."

"What is it? I think you could tell me just about anything and I'd still be happy with you right now, Jasper. I wouldn't normally admit it, but I'm happy I'm not alone."

"They have my sister."

"Who?" Emery said, sitting up.

"Camp Carce. I like to think I would have been persistent with you to go, anyway. But I can't know for sure, because I have to go get her." He said, looking out the skylight at the stars.

"We will save her." Emery said, reaching over and putting her hand on his arm. Normally it would have felt lovely, but Jasper had to pretend it didn't hurt from the injuries he gave himself when he was upset earlier.

"But I feel bad for not telling you. I feel bad for having this ulterior motive."

"It doesn't always matter why you do something. It matters that you do it."

"It's my fault." He choked tears into his throat. "She is a flamethrower because of me. I didn't know how to use my power and I accidentally burned her. I didn't tell you the whole story. My mom thought I was a demon, and she had priest after priest come to see me. One gave me a full, painful exorcism. I cried out from my bed afterwards as my mom spoke to the priest downstairs. She came to let me go, and I burned her. It wasn't long before Camp Carce came to kidnap us both. My mom didn't even cry. She smiled as they shot both of us with a tranquilizer. I didn't mean to Emery. I swear I didn't mean to."

"Sounds like we need some training then." She said, smiling at him then getting sad by his tears laying behind his eyes, not even within them. "I turned Levi into one. I didn't mean to either. That's why you're right, Jasper. We do need to train. But right now we need to rest, our time's going to come." She said, pulling her hand off his arm before turning around and cuddling into her chair. They both stayed up for a little while, struggling to get comfortable and with the thought of sleeping after revealing their biggest mistakes. Then once those thoughts drifted, they couldn't sleep because they both knew how impossible the next day seemed. Then finally they couldn't sleep because they were right next to someone they actually liked. Emery thought of what Jasper had said at dinner. She thought about whether or not this car, these woods, and this boy would be the last time she felt this way. So, she finally soaked it in and fell into a deep sleep that could only be followed by a deep test.

When the sun came up, they enjoyed some time in it before they prepared for their next mission. They didn't bring up the kids. They didn't bring up his sister or Levi. They definitely didn't talk about Macy. They needed their strength and these pains all had to be put on hold. Instead, they tried to give themselves what could possibly be their last moments. They talked about their favorite memories and let the time be for just an hour, holding each other's hands. Jasper just finished a story about the time he got stuck in a slide at the park when the familiar silence fell over them. She smiled at him and took her hand out of his.

They both got up knowing what this meant, and I must confess, even I felt quite scared. When they opened the car doors and hopped back inside, they looked at each other again. This time they both looked serious and nodded to each other as Jasper started the car and pulled out of the camp site.

Camp Carce was only another two hours away, and they knew they were getting close as they started up windy roads that Emery remembered from their escape. When they estimated they were almost a mile out, they parked the car. Jasper grabbed a blanket from the back seat and used the steak knife to tear it into pieces.

"We will use them as markers to get back to the car. As soon as we get the kids, we should get as many of them into the car. This time we won't have Philip be in charge of the kids, though. I'm going to bring them to safety this time."

Emery almost cringed at the word safety, which made her remember Elias and his constant affirmations of their safety when they were at His Place Diner.

They started walking up the hill, and Jasper kept tying the cloth onto trees as they passed them. They stopped when they saw Camp Carce's gate and the jeeps all lined up. They knelt behind a large stone. It was terrifying going from one prison to the next and for just a moment, Jasper thought he should probably just run away. But that was an instinct in his human body that was not strong enough to overpower his will to save his sister, the other kids, and ultimately Emery herself.

Emery whispered, "They don't seem to have power besides the cooling mechanism and the physical strength of the Keepers themselves. I think if we can turn the cold off again, we will be able to move. Then once we release kids, they will help us. I'll go in first. I have a way to turn off the system hopefully. I'll send fire out as a sign when it's clear. You come in and start releasing the children while I take care of the staff."

"Got it. I'm waiting for your fire signal. I'll go in closer with you." Jasper looked back at Emery. "Be careful." They both leaned in and had their first kiss. To both of their surprise, an actual spark leapt out from their kiss and they both pulled back, smiling like they never had before.

"I will." Emery said, starting to sneak forward with Jasper following but from a distance. When she got to the gate, she burned a hole in it big enough to crawl through and she looked back one last time at Jasper's eyes that she could see peeking behind a tree at her. Jasper watched the man at the gate, who had not even noticed and instead was almost literally nose-deep in a magazine of some sort.

She crawled in and then ran while crouched to behind one of the cars. She was looking around it, determining her next move. When Jasper noticed from the distance Estrella and two large Keepers coming outside and going right towards the car that Emery was hiding behind. Emery went to crawl under the car and to the other side when the tree Jasper had been hiding by was suddenly aflame.

She panicked and moved towards the back of the car as she saw Estrella and the two Keepers started running in the direction of the flame. They had barely begun, and the plan was up in flames. She couldn't go back for Jasper now, especially since he had successfully gotten Estrella and 2 Keepers away, which she had quickly realized was his plan. She needed to trust that part of that plan was also to get away before they got to the tree. She spotted the door the three had come from and made a run for it. The door from the outside to inside was locked, and she quickly jumped to the side of it as it opened.

She grabbed it quickly and snuck in. She closed it slowly so they wouldn't notice. When she turned around, she faced Dave, the other gate keeper holding a coffee mug and a newspaper. She wanted to pull her hands up to start a fire before he would drench them both, but she was surprised when he started talking casually.

"Emery, right?"

"Right" She felt no harm in denying it. She was either going to have to light him on fire or be captured within the next few moments and neither of those outcomes would be different with any other name than Emery.

"They talk about you constantly here."

"Oh," she said awkwardly, slowly allowing the heat to travel from her body to her hands, prepared to make her move at any moment.

"Will you get that door for me?" He said, motioning to the door with his newspaper.

She turned and opened the door and watched him walk out. When she took her hand off the doorknob, she realized she had almost completely melted it. She was confused but also didn't have time to analyze her luck and she certainly didn't imagine she would be as lucky with the other Keepers at Camp Carce.

She still took a moment to delight in her first real luck in many years. But she didn't have much time. So she kept making her way through the doors. She was hoping to find her dad to see if he could help her turn off the emergency system. She knew all the halls full of rooms lead to the cafeteria, and all she needed was to get to that cafeteria.

The walk there was nerve wrecking and she noticed her legs were shaking. It was just a hall with doors sealed shut on each side. Nowhere to hide if someone walks around a corner or out of a door. She kept her eyes on the first split in the hallway, where she could at least run or hide behind a wall. But until then, she felt as if she was walking naked through a school and all she could do was pray that none of the doors opened. One step at a time. One door at a time, I whispered from very far away.

She crept by and finally made it to the end of the hall, where it split into three halls. She looked around the corner and saw three Keepers talking in the hall.

"Jerry said that the whole crew is out there looking for him. I heard Estrella is basically on fire. She is so mad." He chuckled a bit at this last part.

"Do they know who it is?"

"No, but they are thinking one of those kids that escaped the inescapable camp."

A beeping started going off on one of their watches that made Emery jump. She watched the three of them suddenly get very straight faces on. They all walked to different doors that were near them and opened them up. She watched two kids walk out in old dirty clothes from each room. She crouched down as low as she could against the wall as the Keepers walked the kids past her hallway.

She jumped up as the last kid followed and caught a glimpse of Emery watching from around the corner. She quickly moved back against the wall but couldn't help but peek out again at the boy. It was a boy around seventeen who looked completely in shock. His face turned red. Not in an embarrassed way, but in a way that made her feel like it might shoot up in flames. She put her finger to her lips in a shh signal. She waited till they got closer to her hallway and joined the six kids as they walked by. She pushed her way into the middle of them, and although the kids noticed they didn't dare to breathe a word, not because they were aware that she was there to save them, but because they were simply too scared of the Keepers to say a word.

They lead them to the lunchroom and Emery was so relieved. This was exactly what she needed and so far she hadn't needed to light anyone on fire. With that thought, she pictured Macy up in flames again and shuddered. She had to go save the other children and adults. How would she possibly beat someone as powerful as Elias, though? She physically pinched herself. She had to focus. She went and sat at a table filled with other teens, keeping her head low. The cafeteria staff started coming out with trays, and she desperately searched for her dad. A girl at the table with large brown curly hair whispered, "Hey are you new?"

Emery leaned in, as all the teens did. "I'm releasing you all. Be ready to fight."

Without any other context, the teens all looked at her like she was weird. She remembered the first time she escaped and how the teens had been just as reluctant then. So she looked at the other kids in the cafeteria while her table continued whispering as if nothing had happened, and as if Emery was not even there.

Even there, in this moment of fear and desperation, this stung her. She hadn't quite escaped the mortification that so easily triggered in her, especially when she was around other teenagers. She pinched herself. She had to focus. Jasper was waiting for her somewhere. She just knew it. She focused and searched the faces of workers only to not see her dad, Joaquin, anywhere. She would have to take a chance. When one walked up to their table and put a tray in front of her.

"Is Joaquin here?" Emery asked quietly.

The woman looked alarmed, then whispered back.

"Joaquin hasn't worked here for a while." Then she scurried away into the back. That was that. She had no idea what she would do now. She was counting on her dad to be there. She looked at the food in defeat. She couldn't help but let intrusive thoughts flood her.

Jasper was probably dead. There was no way he escaped them for this long. Even if he did and entered the building, the safety wasn't turned off and they would capture and kill him, anyway. Her dad? Her dad was probably equally as dead. She would be captured herself after lunch and no kids would escape. Elias would burn the other children, ever single one of them, before moving on to the adults. Then he would probably go into the world and turn more people into flame-throwers, just to murder them too. She shook it off even if deep down she thought the darkest things she had to keep going. She had to light a lantern and look for more light wherever she could find it because, in this moment, she was their only chance.

Lunch ended and the kids all got up and went to the door. She wasn't sure what was next, but she piled into the middle. But as soon as Keepers started putting kids back into their rooms, they would surely notice she wasn't supposed to be there, so she had to think fast. They started walking to doors. They all walked out and started following Keepers down the hall as they began dropping kids off in their cells. Each door that two kids entered her heart grew darker. She would just have to light the Keepers up once they noticed and make a run for it.

Another door, another moment closer.

Another door, another fear entered her.

They were down to about six kids, and they would surely notice soon. Her hands glowed red behind her back and she pushed herself to come up with a plan, any plan. She would light their shoes up. Maybe they could melt and maybe they wouldn't go up in flames. Maybe they wouldn't call for help in time, and she could steal their keys. Her red hands began to feel hot against her skin.

A hand grabbed her elbow and pulled her into a room as they passed it. It was over. They had failed. Her hands immediately went up in flames. She knew one thing, she would fight until there was nothing of her left. They would have to burn her to ashes like Emily if they were going to get her to stop.

"Whoa, whoa it's just me."

Phillip stood in front of her, backing up to the wall of the room he pulled her into.

"Phillip!" She hugged him and wasn't sure why. She never particularly liked Phillip. But just a familiar face after the past 30 minutes of non-breathing and a train of fears, was a relief.

"What are you doing here?" He asked. She looked around the room. It wasn't like the other rooms. This looked like a typical teenager's room in every way. He had a TV and a big green beanbag in front of it. He had a large bed with lights strung all around it and pictures on the wall of famous women she had seen in magazines.

"What's going on here Phillip?"

"They captured us Emery, me and the kids. But when I returned, they offered me a job. They want me to make sure no other escapes happen, and they said would set me up nicer." He said which was the script he wrote down five times when he saw Emery in the cameras of the cafeteria. He was proud that he recited it much more naturally than he thought he would be able to.

"Well, I don't think that they picked the right person for that job, Phillip. You ready to be fired?" Emery responded.

"Always." He said smiling and reaching out for her hand, which she pulled back.

"We need to release the other kids. I need to turn off the safety and open the doors. This is a big one Phillip."

"If I do this. If I take you to the security room and help you. What can I get in return?"

She noted to herself that Phillip was someone she hoped one day to never see again. She also noted that something seemed very strange about his new job and one day, to find the truth. But she knew today was not the day and today she needed him.

"Freedom from all this. We found a nicer place where we can all be happy. Together." She smiled sweetly, yet had never felt more disgusting inside.

"Ok come on."

He pushed her back as he opened the door and looked around. He grabbed her hand and walked her through the hallways as both barely breathed. They got to a large black door. He took out some keys and opened it. He pushed her to the left side of the door so that when it opened, the Keeper wouldn't see her. She overheard Phillip talking to a Keeper on the other side of the door.

"Hey Alec."

"Phillip."

"Estrella said she needs you now for that fire in the woods."

"Why wouldn't she radio me?"

"He burned it apparently."

"Fuck me. Ok but I need you to stay here. Earlier I saw a spark of flame on this screen. Push the safety button if there are any more."

"Got it."

The Keeper walked out, and Emery held her breath as he opened the door and walked away. She held it and walked into the room with Phillip. He was at the computers, punching in some codes to disable the system. She looked at the walls of the room and saw tons of jeep car keys hung on them. She started putting them all in her pocket, one by one.

"Ok safety is disabled."

"We need to open the doors too, Phillip."

"I can get you out of here again, Emery. But opening the doors to the rooms makes no sense. Honestly, it's dangerous. There are tons of kids here and you have to believe me, they are dangerous."

"I need you to open the doors." Emery said firmly.

Phillip turned to her. "Emery, once we open these doors there is no going back. This isn't like last time where you had a plan in a small area. This is all the children, all the doors. Some could be right next to Keepers. Some could be dangerous."

"Is the speaker system in here as well?"

"Ya." He said, pointing to the intercom. Dreading his future, but too infatuated with Emery to say no.

"I'm going to make an announcement. You make the doors open. Then I'm going to run through make sure kids get out safely. I need you to go outside and shoot a flame into the air."

"For what?"

"For Jasper, he is in the woods waiting."

"You brought Jasper?"

She ignored the question and started tossing him the rest of the car keys she had found. "Give these to kids old enough to drive as you see them. Tell them to take as many kids as they can and meet us at the end of the road."

She leaned into the intercom and turned it on. She put her hand on his shoulder and gave him a nod.

She cleared her throat, and it could be heard in the whole building.

"Today, Camp Carce dies. Today, you will need to fight. Security is down. Be brave. Light it up. "

She nodded to Phillip, and he pressed the button to release the doors. They ran out of the room and Emery burned the front of the door so that it couldn't be opened again. Two Keepers immediately started running towards them and she burned a wall of fire right in front of them as she and Phillip ran the other way. Kids started peering out into the hallway from the rooms.

Emery and Phillip yelled as they ran, "Run guys! Light it up!" More kids started coming into the hallway, some with hands on fire. Emery started throwing the older one's car keys.

"Phillip, I need you to go get Jasper."

Phillip went off in a different direction. As Emery ran

through the halls, creating fire walls whenever she saw keepers and leading kids out towards one of the side doors. The kids weren't doing much, but shuffling and running at first. But the kids started throwing fireballs at Keepers once the Keepers started grabbing children one by one. She watched a child almost light on fire herself in a Keeper's arms and the Keeper let go and started rolling across the floor desperately.

Phillip was doing the exact same in the other hallway. He would not be going to get Jasper. One because he hated Jasper, and he hated the way that he saw Jasper look at Emery when they had all been together. Two, because he had still not really come clean to Emery. He didn't have any fire power at all. When he had been taken to Camp Carce, this was exactly what they were looking for, a dumb teen that couldn't defend himself should he ever need to. Most of this time, his lack of fire power made him feel weak and sad. He even considered once asking a kid to burn him if he helped them. But watching them all suffer while he hung out in his room watching court shows always reminded him he preferred the life of the helpless little spy. He hoped that just this time, his lack of power was a good thing and that maybe it would get Jasper killed.

The hallways were filled with flame now and Keepers desperately tried to grab kids like they were trying to desperately hit at like mosquitos. Emery turned a corner and saw a Keeper grab a little girl, who screamed.

"Use your fire!" She yelled, but the little girl just cried. Emery shot fire out at the Keeper's feet and he collapsed to the ground. She ran and grabbed the kid and started heading to the door where the cars were waiting.

When she reached the final door, she saw a massive Keeper and Estrella standing right in front of them. Emery let the little girl down and pushed her behind her with the two other teens that had followed them down the hall and were now waiting, terrified, behind Emery.

"I should have known you were behind this Emery." Estrella said while rolling up her sleeves and showing her colorful snake. "I knew you would be back. No....I hoped. I hoped you would be back Emery. We had barely just begun our work with you.

"Estrella, I need you to move."

"I developed something since your last time here." She pulled out a small little bottle that looked like a lipstick.

"With the help of science this takes away your powers. It's not perfect, of course. I don't quite know if it's forever or for a few moments. I do know it's quite painful, which is just an unexpected perk of course. If all I have from all of this is you. "She pointed with the bottle right at Emery. "I'm more than happy to take it. I could lose all of them. I just need you."

"Last warning Estrella."

"Oh Emery, always so confident. I am not the one who needs the warning." She opened the small bottle in her hands and Emery's whole arms lit on fire. She couldn't block this door with a fire wall. Too many of the kids need it. Suddenly she felt more heat coming from her back. But something felt different this time. It didn't feel like the heat she had become so used to. She turned around and saw Jasper and about ten more kids were behind her, all with flames in their hands.

Jasper moved forward and stood next to Emery before

she could stop him. Estrella opened the cap and threw it to-wards Emery and Jasper and it hit Jasper and burned his skin blue. Estrella looked amazed and unsure if she failed or not, as Jasper's yells rang through the hall. She quickly grabbed the Keeper and put him in front of her, as she looked at the remaining teens all with fire in their hands and Emery with fire seeming coming lightly from every pore on her body. She looked at Emery, then made a run for it right out the door.

"Get to the cars!" Emery yelled as she got down on the ground with Jasper. "Are you ok Jasper?"

He shuttered in pain. "I'm ok." He pulled his hand out wanting a flame, but nothing came. "It's ok, come on." She said pulling him up with the help of two other teen boys and they limped him out to the car. They got Jasper into one of the jeeps and the cars all started with last minute kids running and jumping in, all piling on top of each other into cars. Emery shut the car door as she got Jasper into it. "What are you doing?"

She looked back at Keepers making their way through flames, now carrying guns. "Go everyone!" She yelled. The jeeps all started and began to drive away. She stood behind facing the Keepers, who now each held guns. She focused. This would be the most difficult thing she had ever tried. She flew out a line of flames burning the guns in their hands. She threw massive balls of fire at the rest of the building and watched some pieces burn and some fight back. A jeep quickly slid behind her and someone opened the door.

"Get in" Phillip yelled, and she jumped in. They closed the door and they sped off to the bottom of the lane where jeeps with screaming children held packed. Phillip drove in front of all of them and motioned for the cars to follow him. The jeeps all drove away in a line as if they had been called to war.

15

Burning Another Door Down

Emery guided Phillip in the right direction. Their plan was to return to His Place Diner but first they needed to stop, get some rest, and come up with a plan. She also had an overwhelming desire to kiss Jasper again, that was filling her body like flames as they drove. The other kids began to fall asleep as Emery and Phillip tried to find a place hidden in the woods that would also hold all their cars.

"Phillip, how did they catch you guys?"

"They recognized the car. We got surrounded as we drove, and I didn't have any choice. They took in all the kids and threatened to hurt them if I put up a fight."

"I'm sorry."

"It's not your fault. But what will make this time different? I don't want to constantly feel like I'm on the run from these people." He looked at Emery. " I want you and I to just be able to rest, not worry about this for the rest of our lives."

"I wish I had better news, but we are still in danger. We found a place where they keep kids and adults. It seemed safe. But." She looked at the other sleeping kids in the car and assumed there might be other Emerys in there, pretending to be asleep, but not actually. So, she chose her words carefully.

"It's not safe. We have to work together to release them, too. Then we will find a safe place. We can plan tonight."

"Ok." Phillip said with clear annoyance in his voice.

Then, after a moment, he put his hand on her knee. She carefully pulled his hand off her knee and looked at him. "Sorry I'm not comfortable with that."

He didn't respond and kept driving straight. They drove a few hours into a dirt road turnoff until they saw a random cabin that looked empty. They stopped the jeep and motioned for everyone else to stop as well. Phillip and Emery got out of the car and multiple teens followed from other jeeps. They all gathered at the front of the line of cars and Jasper came up, moving more slowly than usual, but with a smile on his face as he saw Emery again.

"This one looks empty and secluded. But we have to make sure first. Everyone be careful as we check it out. Don't start any fires, it would give us away and it's too dangerous." Emery said, addressing the new group of teens they had just released.

"Why are you in charge?" Shouted a stocky boy with dark and long hair.

"I'm not, but we have done this before. We have escaped successfully." She decided to not release the information that after they escaped, they were essentially captured again, and she would need these kids' help in saving the others. One fire at a time. Always, one fire at a time. The teenagers began climbing the small hill up to the cabin and surrounded the cabin looking for signs of anyone. They all crouched and whispered as they crept around it. Until, in true Phillip fashion, they heard a massive crash as Phillip broke the front window. A couple of the kids entered the cabin through the window at him and shouted all clear.

The cabin itself was very modern and luxurious. It had about ten rooms, all with the nicest beds and furniture. There was glass everywhere and right in the middle was a massive, beautiful wood fireplace. Emery and Jasper looked around as Phillip ordered the teens back to the jeeps to drive the children to the cabin as well, who were still waiting at the cars. He instructed everyone to try to find somewhere to park that the jeeps wouldn't be noticed.

Emery and Jasper entered the main bedroom that had a large, beautiful window in front of it that showed beautiful trees surrounding them and a wind chime made of all different colors of stones. Jasper first sat on the luxurious white bed covered and light brown detailed wood posts. Then he laid down, still drained from whatever experiment Estrella had thrown at him.

Emery laid down next to him. She felt content for just a moment in the fact that last night likely wasn't her last safe sleep and soaked in the comfort of the bed. Gently, she curled into Jasper and put her arm across his stomach. The door opened and three teen girls walked in giggling and checking the room out.

"Woah, this is the best one." They said, walking around and starting to look through drawers in it. One of the girls, with long blonde hair and a stunning smile that made Emery both jealous and happy for her, said, "Hey! You're Jasper and Emery!"

Emery sat up from the bed and looked to her, "Yes."

"People talk about you guys all the time. Did you actually save us too?"

Emery could not be comfortable answering that question with a yes. She was no savior, and she still hadn't told them that she needed them to help save others.

"We came to get you guys. But we aren't safe just yet."

"Girls come on; this is their room for sure. Let's go snag that upstairs room with the bunk beds in it." The girls shut the drawers and followed her. As she closed the door, she looked at Emery and Jasper.

"I'm Amanda, by the way. There is a lock on this door too." She said, motioning to the door and giving a small smile as she did. Emery was quite relieved to notice the lock. Not for the reasons Amanda had anticipated but because she needed privacy for their next plan. She hadn't really given herself time to celebrate this success, as she was too focused on the next challenge. She smiled and looked down at Jasper, who seemed to have fallen asleep within the past couple of moments. Whatever it was Estrella had worked so hard to develop was powerful and Emery wondered how many she had. She wondered if they could be weaponized. But she couldn't focus on that now. So, she crept out of the room and left Jasper there to sleep.

She was amazed at what she saw when she walked out of the bedroom. Children running around. Teenagers were kissing in the corner. Some kids were laughing, some were crying, but overall, a feeling of joy reached through her bones. This group was different from the first one they escaped with. They had more energy. They must have been feeding off each other and their recent battle with the Keepers. She saw the group of girls from earlier all sitting at the kitchen counter and she walked over to sit with them.

"Hey girl," Amanda said, motioning to an empty chair. She pushed over a wine glass and filled it to the rim with wine. "They found a wine cellar. Don't worry, I have the key so kids can't get it." She sat jingling a small key from her pocket.

"How'd you do it?" Another girl with large glasses asked.

"I had a lot of help." Emery said, taking a drink from the wine. Two more girls who had been upstairs but looked a bit younger came and sat down at the table. One had short brown hair that almost spiked up, with strikingly bright blue eyes, and Emery realized she recognized her as the girl who silenced her at her first lunch at Camp Carce. "I want some."

"Lor, you're literally 14. I don't think so. But you can have a sip of mine." Amanda said, passing the young girl her wine. Lor took the smallest sip and quickly made a disgusted face, passing it back to her.

"Girls, this is Emery. She was part of the group that escaped the first time. She came back to save us."

Emery turned red, this time not from fire. She did not like this type of attention. But it was quickly taken away when Lor accidentally started a small fire on the table. The girls rushed to put it out with a bowl of water from the sink behind them.

"What the fuck Lor?" the girl with the larger glasses asked.

"Sorry guys. I just I don't know. Sometimes my emotion triggers it." Lor said. Emery looked back to Lor and her hands grew red again, but she closed her eyes and took a breath and they calmed.

"Jasper." She said with her eyes closed. Then, slowly open them again slowly. "My brother Jasper. He escaped with the first group. Is he ok?"

"Jasper" Emery smiled. "You're Jasper's sister. He told me about you." She stood up from the table and gave out her hand. Lor took it and followed her to the master bedroom. She opened the door and Jasper rolled over and opened his eyes. Lor collapsed into him, hugging him and crying. Jasper woke up quickly and held her in his arms so tight neither thought he would ever let go. Emery smiled, relieved and started to close the door.

"Wait!" Jasper yelled to Emery without unhanding his sister. "Thank you, Emery." He said and this time he let one tear fall from his face. Emery smiled and nodded, then shut the door to give the siblings some time to gather themselves.

She returned to the table where the girls were still chatting and drinking.

"The boys made a fire pit outside for a fire tonight." Amanda told Emery.

"Cool, that will be fun. I have to tell you guys we have a difficult journey ahead of us."

"What's the plan?" The girl with the large glasses asked.

"We have to go save some more kids."

"More fighting?" Amanda asked.

"More fighting, but I feel like it could be easier than Camp Carce. The only problem is the people at this new place are also flamethrowers."

"Flamethrowers?" Amanda asked.

"That's what people have come to call people like us, people who have fire power like us."

"How are we supposed to fight other flamethrowers?" She asked.

"We have to be better than them. We just have to be smarter than them. But we have some time. First, I think everyone needs rest." She looked out the front window to see boys gathering around a pit. "First, I think you all need some normalcy." Emery suddenly felt incredibly grateful for the glimpses of normalcy she had experienced over the past week. That first campfire with Jasper, laughing in the cabins, eating lunch with her new friends, the second fire with Jasper in her room, the last campfire, the kiss that sparked everything, and the fire she knew would come from it.

"So, if this is the kids you escaped with. Are the other kids, ok?" Amanda asked in a more whispered tone than before.

"Maybe. It's a dangerous place. He already killed one. But for the moment, the other kids don't know. This place also has adults. Some of them are bad, some of them are good."

Amanda shifted. "How do we know who is good and who is bad?"

Emery took another drink of the wine. "Sometimes you don't. Sometimes you just have to assume everyone is good until they show you they are bad."

"I like to assume the opposite." Phillip's voice came in

from directly behind Emery, "Everyone is bad until they show you, they are good." He grabbed one of the wine bottles and took a swig. "They usually don't."

Amanda rolled her eyes. "Thanks for asking Phillip."

"Oh, was this your wine Amanda? I thought it belonged to some random ass cabin owner. But now I understand that while you were at Camp Carce, you made your own wine in that tiny little cell, then held onto it like a baby as we all just fought for our lives to get away." Emery looked back at Phillip sternly and this time they both knew she knew at least one secret that the many flamethrowers would probably be interested in hearing, then he continued, looking straight at her.

"Anyway, the sun is going down, and we found some hot dogs frozen. We are all getting around the fire if you want to join us. Where's Jasper?" He asked Emery accusingly.

"He is in the room."

"Isn't he your boyfriend now?"

Emery felt so uncomfortable to be having this conversation in front of the girls, "No Phillip, he isn't." She got up from her chair and passed by him to the back door.

She saw about 20 kids all in different spots around a large fire out front. She grabbed a seat next to a boy around her age talking to a little girl that she recognized from the first escape. She was telling the boy a story about how she was burned.

"Then the bad man said that it was ok. He said that he was a friend of my mom's. He even knew her name and all. Then he just grabbed me. He held me tight in his arms and started burning me." She put her arms in front of her and showed them both the delicate burns lining her arms. Jasper and Lor walked out through the back door as the little girl showed her scars with Emery arm and arm. They spotted Emery and came to take a seat.

"Hi, I'm Emery." She said, leaning over and shook Lor's hand.

"Lor. Thanks so much Jasper said that you saved us."

"You all saved yourselves." Emery said.

"But we still have work to do."

"He told me that, too. I'm ready to fight." Lor said, sparks coming from her fingers.

Jasper pulled her arm down. "I want you to stay here and wait for us."

"No way Jasper."

"Look, someone needs to watch the kids. We can't take them with us. It's too dangerous."

"What about Phillip?" She said, laughing.

"What do you mean because they got captured again?" Emery asked.

"Oh no, that's not the rumor."

"What's the rumor?" Emery leaned in.

"Ask one of the littles. Marie, what happened when you ran away with Phillip."

They all glanced over at Phillip, who was on the other side of the fire. He was staring right at them. He had a hotdog in the fire but looked just above it and at Emery instead. Something felt sinister in it, even though there was no way he could actually hear what they were saying.

"Phillip brought us right back to Camp Carce. We cried and cried but he said it was all for the best."

"What do you mean I thought you all were captured?" Emery said, staring right back at Phillip through the fire.

"No, no, no, we didn't even see no Keepers till we got back to Camp Carce. Plus, here is the weirdest part. When we got back, the Keepers grabbed all of us besides Phillip. He just stood there watching with Estrella. I don't like him!"

Jasper immediately started to get up, and Emery pushed him back down.

"Cool it Jasper. It won't do any good right now."

He stared at Phillip with anger in his eyes. He took his hand from around Emery and pushed more fire into the flame, lighting Phillip's hotdog and stick on fire. Phillip had to jump back and throw the stick in the pit. Jasper took the moment to be thrilled that his fire was back and that he had ruined even just one thing for Phillip.

"What the fuck?" Phillip said, jumping up and walking towards Jasper. Jasper stood incredibly still and although his hand glowed red, he didn't move a muscle knowing his sister was still right in front of him. When Phillip pushed Emery to the side, Jasper's hands lit up in bigger fire balls than Emery had ever seen. She jumped up too.

"Let's fucking do this Phillip." He looked Phillip up and down and at his hands. Was he so incredibly calm that his hands didn't even glow?

"Where's your flame Phillip?" he said through clenched teeth.

"You're so much of a bitch that you can't just fight without flames Jasper? Plus, I thought you got your ass kicked by little Estrella and couldn't even do shit anymore."

"No, I can't fight without my fire. When flamethrowers are mad, their fire comes. I'm sure you know that already." He stepped forward. "So, what are you, Phillip? I don't see any flames at all."

"I'm not a weak ass kid relying everything on their powers. How about that?" Phillip said, stepping closer slowly.

"If you ever go near my sister or Emery again, I'll burn you to a crisp." Jasper said with his teeth still clenched.

Emery came back with Amanda and the girls she had met all carrying buckets of water. Emery set hers down and stood between the boys, facing Jasper.

"He isn't worth it, Jasper. You have to be a leader. We have people to save."

Jasper took one last look at Phillip, then fell into the eyes of Emery. He looked down at his hands, aflame.

"Emery I can't put them out."

"I know."

She motioned for Amanda, who walked up and poured the bucket of water on Jasper. Smoke emerged from him and his eyes looked almost blank once he looked up again. Drenched wet, he walked away as Phillip scoffed as if he had won. What he wasn't expecting was to turn around to see a large kid with ring nose piercing named Blake, standing behind him now with his own hands on fire.

"You're a snitch. You can't be here. You been lying to us all this whole time. We had a feeling." Lor got up and said, "Blake stop."

Phillip punched the kid, and the kid hit him with a fireball.

One of the girls with the water poured it out on him, but you could still smell his flesh burning. More teens with glowing red hands started to run towards Phillip on the ground.

Suddenly, a massive explosion and ball of light from the fire pit shot some kids back and silenced everyone. Emery stood in front of the pit as it came down. "Stop! We don't have time for this, and it's not the right thing to do. We have to save this anger. We are all headed to a bad place called His Place Diner." She took a breath and threw another large light into the fire to keep their attention. "There are more flame-throwers, and we owe it to them to save them too. We didn't escape from this to destroy ourselves. Phillip go inside. Some-one go take care of him. Everyone else take a seat. This is our last relaxing night. Tomorrow we have to fight. After that, we have to find somewhere safe. We need each other."

Kids reluctantly all started returning to seats and the girl with the big glasses followed Phillip inside to help him with his injury. The feelings weren't the same the rest of the night and terror and anger held in the air, between forced laughs and stories.

Eventually, they discussed the plan to save the other children in more detail. People who were too scared volunteered to stay behind with the kids. People who were just waiting for a new fight were silently thrilled to put their powers to use again. Once they agreed who stayed and who would go, Emery had to make sure they knew exactly what they were getting into. Emery told the kids about Elias and his burning Macy to become more powerful. They were scared but also strangely interested in knowing more about their own powers, and some of them were most interested in saving the others that were in danger.

As the night drew on the teens and kids all went their separate ways. Some of them were sleeping, some were kissing, but most of them were crying. But Emery and Lor stayed by the fire talking and swapping tales of Jasper, when he walked up behind them from drying off and cooling down.

"Pretty intense Jasper." Lor said.

"It's been a very intense week Lor and also I'm beyond sick of that dude."

"Ya, you and Blake just couldn't hold it together. I get it. But, we could probably still use him tomorrow." Lor said, rolling her eyes.

"Well, I don't want him staying here with you and the kids, so it's our only option, anyway."

"I'm not staying here, Jasper. I'm going with Emery and you to fight Elias."

Jasper quickly looked at Emery, and she felt his eyes on her.

"I thought she should stay too, Jasper. I don't know what else to say." Emery said, putting her hands closer to the fire as if she was cold.

"Look Lor, I don't think you get it. This guy is bad. He burned our friend right in front of us, just to steal her power for a moment. It's dangerous."

"I understand that."

"What if he burned a regular human?" Emery asked, looking towards Jasper in almost a trance from visualizing the murder again.

"I don't think anything would happen." Jasper answered, still kind of closed off.

"Is he as powerful as you?" She asked Emery.

"He is when he does that."

"Then why are you that powerful? Have you killed some flamethrowers before?" Lor asked with a hint of an attitude.

"No, I don't know why I'm this way."

Then Blake came over and asked Lor to take a walk with him. She smiled and got up. Jasper went to say something but stopped himself and looked at Emery.

"Not my fuckin night I guess."

"Well, maybe it is." Emery said, a bit shy. "I was thinking we could share the master. It seems to be ok with everyone and I don't know. You're the only one I trust to not kill me anymore."

"I hope you say that in our wedding vows one day." He laughed, pretending to be standing at an altar with his hand out as he continued. "You're the only person I can trust to not kill me anymore." he mimicked people in a crowd saying "Awww" like it was romantic.

She laughed and got up and hit him at his side.

"I asked to share a room not get married. Let's just stay alive together first."

"You got it." Jasper said, looking Emery in the eyes now.

"First stay alive together, next spend our lives together." He said giving her a new wink she hadn't gotten before.

Emery smiled, and they went inside to the master bedroom to relax just the two of them and watch some TV. Emery fell asleep laying on Jasper. He looked at her and this time he pulled her hair back. It was much softer than he ever imagined, and he wanted to cherish that moment. For a moment, he didn't want to go back for the others. He wanted to just stay in this moment, just the two of them. They had already put out the fire of Camp Carce and ran away. They defeated Elias and escaped; they freed the children, why couldn't they just rest now? Why was there always another fire to put out?

He fell asleep with these thoughts. But he woke up ready to put another fire out. He had only needed some rest to realize each challenge was one challenge closer to normalcy. It's funny what a night of sleep will do to someone, isn't it? Jasper rolled over and saw Emery looking up at the ceiling and soaked in a new day, a new challenge, and one more step to her.

"Morning." She said, looking at him.

"Morning. You ok?"

"Yes, I'm just ready. I can't stop thinking about what he did to Macy now and I can't wait to put my hands on him." Her hands became red and shined in the room. Jasper pulled one of her hot hands up to his lips and kissed them. She watched and both of her hands turned back down to a regular color.

"We will take him. But together. I think I've made it pretty clear since day one that we are going to be in this together. Putting your hands on Elias won't work and you know it, we have to combine our powers."

"I know. But I don't think that that will be enough Jasper." She sighed. "I had another idea too." She turned towards him. "We leave two cars here just in case. We only need about 2 cars for those of us going to fight. Let's take the gasoline from the other cars."

"The gasoline?"

"Ya, the boys found water guns downstairs. We fill them up with gasoline. Then anyone can spray it to create a wall like I do."

"I love it. Even worse, what happens if a flamethrower tries to use their power with gasoline on them? I can't imagine anything good."

"I didn't think of that. We should warn people not to directly spray flamethrowers unless it's an emergency. We don't need any more surprises."

"And Phillip? What are we going to do about Phillip?" Jasper said, rolling onto his back and looking at the ceiling now.

"I'm going to take care of Phillip."

"Oh, please let me take care of Phillip Emery. I am very interested in having that position here. I probably won't even kill him." He chuckled.

"Just trust me." Emery said, getting out of bed and putting her hoodie on and putting her hair up. Jasper watched her and said, "Can I have another kiss, Emery?" She put her hood up over her head and jumped back onto the bed. "Yes." She said this time with conviction. He pulled her in close and kissed her with more passion this time. Sparks started shooting from both of them, but they didn't stop until a blue flame started to grow in between their bodies. They both pulled back and swatted out the flames. They both laughed though, and Emery got back up and fixed her hair.

She left the room and Jasper took in those moments as deeply as he could. Emery saw the girls sitting around a brand-new fire and went to join them. They whispered in panicked ways and the girl with the large glasses was crying.

"What's wrong?"

Emery put her hand on the girl and almost began to cry a bit.

"What is it?"

"Last night," the girl said between tears. "Blake killed himself."

"What do you mean how, what?" Emery changed her focus quickly to Lor to see if she was ok. She noticed her head down, hood up, and she was wiping her face with her sleeve. Emery walked over to her and put her arm around her.

"I'm so sorry Lor. I could tell you two were close."

"It was awful, Emery. When he asked to take a walk with me. He told me how badly he wanted to kill Phillip. How embarrassed he was that Phillip punched him. I told him it was ok. I told him that no one thought anything more of it. He tried to kiss me, but I denied him. Then I came to the camp and sat around the fire with the girls. But he never he never came back."

Amanda interjected, as Lor was having a hard time finishing what she was saying. "Then when Tad went out to use the bathroom, he found Blake. He lit himself on fire. All that was left was his charred body. Blake was always sad." She put one hand on the girl with large glasses and one hand on Lor. "This isn't anyone's fault." Amanda said. "What you did was right. You have a right to say no to a kiss. He would have done this no matter what. No matter where we were or what we were doing. You can't blame yourself."

Emery was shocked by all this news and felt quite heart-broken for Lor, but she also just didn't have time for it. She was capable of feeling feelings, especially loss. But she had more people to save, and she couldn't save Blake anymore. That was just the reality. "Lor, why don't you go inside to the master bedroom and spend some time with Jasper. Tell him what happened." Lor did a few more sniffles and then went inside as Emery had asked.

After Lor left, Emery stood on top of the cooler and called everyone over. "I know that we have had a loss. I hope you all don't think I'm insensitive to this all. This was a loss and I know you need to grieve. But we also must move forward. I don't know Blake well. But what I do know is he was planning on fighting with us today. So, I need us all to fight together. We will go to The Diner. Free the others and then find our place to breathe. Find our place to grieve. I need those going to fight with us today to prepare yourselves. We will leave in about 30 minutes. We can do this. The fire within you is waiting for freedom, and it's strong enough to fight for it. I promise."

Amanda reached up and helped Emery down.

"Where is Phillip?"

"In the hammock over there. He is still hurt. But he hasn't left the hammock. I think he knows there are people here who would like to see him burned." Amanda said, pointing to an old blue hammock hanging about twenty feet away and slightly swinging.

"Do you trust me?" Emery asked.

"Sure."

"Let's take a walk Amanda."

The two started walking off and walked in the direction of the hammock. Emery began talking as they walked by the hammock.

"I need to tell you the real plan, but the others can't know. There is a rock at the top of this hill. Let's go there. No one can hear us there."

They kept walking, "Ok is everything ok?"

"Yes."

Amanda whispered now. "I heard Phillip get out of the hammock. He might be following us."

Emery grabbed her hand and squeezed it a bit, then continued talking.

"I know that's what they want, but we have to compromise." They made it to the rock at the top and Emery felt assurance in the small rustling noise she heard behind them.

"We are all not really going to fight. We will be safe there. His Place Diner is actually a beautiful safe haven for people like us. But I couldn't let people know. People like Phillip can't know what we are really doing. By tonight we will all be safely at the diner."

"But I don't understand why pretend we are going there to free them?"

"Because not everyone can know the plan. I just don't trust people. Phillip can't be the only bad one and we have to get everyone safely there first."

"Why are we leaving the children here?" Amanda asked, sensing that Emery was lying but still genuinely confused about what she was talking about.

"They will be safe here. The diner ordered complete protection over them. As soon as we leave, they will arrive. Traitors like Phillip will be burned, and we will be safe. We will leave in 30, but only to get supplies. We will arrive safely at His Place Diner tonight around 4pm. I need you to be one of the drivers. It's straight down this road to 225. Then take that south for 2 hours. Turn right onto the dirt road, then you'll see a small sign that says diner ahead. Go the opposite direction and you'll find the diner, a big beautiful shiny white and blue restaurant."

"Ok, I can do that. But I still think we should tell the others." Amanda said, still clearly confused but attempting her best to play along.

More rustling happened behind them, and Emery looked around to see Phillip running frantically down the hill.

"We have to stop him." Amanda said.

"No, we really don't. It was all a ruse Amanda. We still have to go fight. I had to get rid of Phillip."

"I'm afraid I don't quite understand."

"I haven't lied to anyone. I'm sorry for confusing you. I had to send Phillip in the wrong direction."

They looked behind them and headed down the hill as they started hearing yelling and some balls of fire.

"Go get the girls with buckets of water. We are going to have to put these out." Emery said calmly. She walked around to the front and yelled for everyone to stop. They were throwing fireballs at one of the jeeps that Phillip must have hot-wired and was now driving away in.

"Let him go. We have bigger things to do, I promise!" Emery yelled as she came down the hill. "Stop please!" Most of the teens stopped throwing fireballs, leaving only two who didn't stop, but their fireballs weren't enough to stop him. They all put their hands down slowly, and their flames began to go out. They knew they would have a chance soon to release all their pent-up pain and anger; they knew as always there was still another fight to win.

16

Burn It Down

The teens all got ready. Jasper put his foot down and made it clear that Lor would be staying. Lor sat on the stairs up to the cabin with bright red hands and her bright blue eyes staring blankly at a wall. Emery couldn't help but worry she would accidentally set the stairs on fire. So as the teens packed up, Emery sat down next to her and put her hand on her back.

"You have to work on calming down, Lor. I know how difficult it is, but our powers aren't easily controlled if we are angry."

"You have to tell Jasper I can go with you guys."

"We really need you here, Lor. I know this has all been a lot. I know that you lost Blake last night and that you're scared. But someone strong has to be here to protect the kids. I agree with Jasper here. I think if anything, your position is more important than ours. What if they come here? What if they attack," A little boy walked up the stairs past them and Emery began to whisper, "They aren't as strong as us, they need you. I need you." She brushed her hand up and down Lor's back, "Take ten deep breaths allowing yourself to be upset, then take one more, allowing you to be calm and strong."

"I'll do it." Lor said. Emery got up and went to go help the jeeps get lined up to leave.

Then once everyone was ready and, in the jeeps, Emery and Jasper met at the front of the jeep.

"Lor is mad at me." Jasper said. Emery leaned in and gave him a kiss, which again sent a spark flying. She smiled and put it out with her foot.

"We are almost there, Jasper. You made the right choice. We will be back before you know it."

They squeezed each other's hands, then went around to the doors at the front of the jeeps and jumped in. Emery sat in the front seat of one of the jeeps as Jasper drove and the girl with large glasses and Amanda sat in the back seat.

After they drove for about twenty minutes, Jasper put his hand on Emery's knee, and she let it remind her to breathe. It was this breath that made someone who was hiding in the trunk feel kind of uncomfortable as she watched from the side of the back seat. Emery didn't quite like the look of it. So she sat up and looked back.

"Are we powerful enough to take these guys down?" Lor asked from the large, attached trunk area of the jeep.

"Holy shit." Jasper said, swerving a bit and looking back to the cars following them.

"Lor, what the fuck?"

"I'm already here Jasper. Teens younger than me are in the other cars. I came, we are too far to go back. Get over it." She said, now crawling up from the trunk into one of the open seats in the back.

His hands glowed red on the steering wheel. This time

Emery put her hand on his knee, but his red hands didn't grow dull this time.

"So again," Lor said, "Are we even powerful enough to fight these guys?"

"Well, we have the gasoline too. But we just need to de-mobilize them enough to give others a chance to escape. It's not like the other facility; it's not fireproofed. We can burn more, it's just the security that can also burn that is the concerning part." Emery responded, also knowing it was too late to turn back around.

"Why don't we just overrun it and stay there." Lor asked.

"It's too dangerous." Jasper said through clenched teeth.

"What do they do there? Besides murder people, I got that."

"I don't really know. It's pretty luxurious. They have a lot of money and can have anything they want. But I think Elias kills them off and sends other people out to do bad things."

"So, we should rob them too, right? Find the money?" Lor said.

"Lor." Jasper interjected, "Stop. We are just saving the others; you shouldn't even be here. Stay out of the way. I'm serious." He said, looking at her in the rearview mirror.

"I understand that. You guys are the rescuers, we get it. But we need to build a future too and I'm going to take care of us there. I'm going to help us all build a safe future. You guys are living too in the now."

"That's fine Lor. It's good to think about our future." Emery said, moving her hand to put it on Jasper's, which he had moved to the middle area after calming down a bit.

They started to get closer, and he pulled the jeep over to

the side of the road and the other cars followed suit. The kids all got out of the car. They all gathered together.

"Remember these people are flamethrowers too." Jasper said. "Be careful. I need each of you to watch out for Elias. He is more powerful than others. He is a tall man in all black with black slicked hair. If he can get his hands on you." He paused and looked right at Lor. "He will burn you completely to ash and steal your power, which he will use to kill us."

Emery walked up and held Jasper's hand as she now spoke, "Some people might not want to leave, convince them they are unsafe. We will get who we can. Some people worship this man, and they will fight for him. Use your fire and use the gas to form walls. As long as no one is there, you can burn it down. This facility is much more flammable than Camp Carce. Jasper and I will go first, fall behind us, enter together but calmly, not like we are walking in to fight. Lor fall back, you should be last."

Lor's cheeks blushed in only the way a sibling who was continuing to feel like the weak link because of her brother's protective nature of her. Between us, she also still remembered vividly that it was her brother's fault she was like this, anyway. It was her brother's fault that she was now destined to be a warrior.

"Let's go." Emery said confidently.

Do you remember that door? The door of Emery's that I told you at the very beginning was opening for her? Well, that door was about to slam shut.

The teens all walked behind Jasper and Emery as quietly as

possible as His Place Diner came into view through the trees. The group of teens all got in closer behind Jasper and Emery, with Lor still in the very back.

Jasper and Emery slowly opened the front door of the diner and stepped inside while bells rang out in the diner. Amanda and the girl with large glasses stood behind them and held the door open. The waitress, Stacy, who held a plate in her hands, froze when she saw Jasper and Emery. She set the plate down slowly on the table she was in front of, then she pulled her hands up, filled with fire.

The diners noticed and one by one stood with their hands on fire staring at the group of kids. Emery put her hands up but not on fire, although a light red did glow. "We aren't here to fight. We just want to see Elias. Please take me to him, Stacy, and I promise no one will be hurt." Emery remembered her bleeding feet and decided to add, "We can make things much better for you, Stacy." The waitress looked at her skeptically, then motioned to Eric who was one of the diners. "Go get Elias fast." Eric disappeared into the elevator.

"We are burning this diner down." Emery said, drastically changing her tone to more stern once she knew that Elias was on the way. She looked left and right at the diners, particularly taking note of the one young child with a lot of freckles sitting with her mother. "You have 30 seconds to leave the diner. We are saving everyone. If you want to come with us. Fight with us. If you don't. Run."

The mother that Emery noticed picked up her child, and ran out of the diner past the kids, as they all moved out of the way to allow them to pass. Amanda and two girls started spraying their gasoline guns down the diner floors. When the smell of gasoline became incredibly pungent in His Place Diner, another few patrons ran out. A couple stood up and flames started in their hands, and their eyes looked dead or frozen.

"Careful." Emery motioned to the gas.

The elevator opened and Elias walked out all alone with flames coming off every part of his large and intimidating body.

"Do they know Elias?" Emery asked calmly

"Know what exactly, Emery?"

"That you kill the people who live here for extra power."

"Don't we both?" He sniffed in the room, "Smells like you're ready to kill these people right now. I've never done anything like this." He said, looking sternly at the remaining flamethrowers on his side in the diner.

"No. I've come to get my friends and anyone else who wants to leave."

"Perfect, because you've been on my mind quite a lot, Emery. I've thought a lot about it and have come to the conclusion that I'm looking forward to killing you." He walked forward.

"I don't think you could even if you tried."

She looked him straight in his orange eyes and turned around. She pushed past the teens and ran back outside. Elias immediately ran after her, shoving past the teens in the door. The teens looked back, and Jasper yelled. "Stay focused guys, get in the elevator, clear every floor. Meet at the cars." He said, while setting the two rows of gasoline on fire. Then he ran towards the elevator with a couple teens. Some more stayed in the diner and dodged and threw fire balls as the building had small fires growing everywhere.

Outside was a much larger battle of fire. Elias ran at Emery as almost a ball of fire himself and narrowly missed as she fell to the ground.

"How could you do this to these people, Elias? How could you do this to kids?"

She yelled as she threw flames towards his feet that made him fall to the ground.

"You did this. Didn't you burn Levi yourself? That one is on you Emery!"

"It was an accident." She said, stumbling to the side as he started putting a circle of fire around her.

"Nothing is ever really an accident. You are going to kill all those kids. Just because you can't trust anyone. You can't just let people be happy."

"That isn't happiness." She said, shooting such a powerful fire ball out that it put out part of the fire he had created around her and walked out of it. Kids and adults started running from the diner. Some threw fire balls at them while others just ran. Soon she saw both Amanda and Kella run out. Elias turned and lit a large fire in front of those trying to escape. Jasper came out and sprayed Elias down with gasoline as others tried desperately to put out enough of the fire to escape.

Elias went up in flames in a moment, and it caused an explosion that made Emery fall back. Jasper put his hands up and ran over to her to cover her. Elias was now just a ball of fire, and little was left of his human body. After a few moments, he started to calm and become human again. He stood over Jasper and Emery, as Jasper was trying to shield them with his own fire. The waitress and Lor ran over, almost pushing each other, but didn't get much closer as Elias towered over the two of them.

"Well, thank you Jasper. I have never felt more powerful." His flames now were blue, as they combined with Jaspers and the gasoline. Jasper and Emery rolled to the side as Elias threw a fireball at them. Emery struggled to get up, and Jasper followed her. Jasper stood in front of her, but she pulled him behind and lit her arms with flames.

But before Emery could shoot a fire at Elias. A large light of fire was just to the side. Jasper and Emery looked over to see what happened. The waitress, Stacy, was down on her knees screaming as Lor burned her body until it turned completely black and fell to the ground. The fire crawled up her arms, and she grew a bit and turned and shot a large fireball at Elias that pushed him back onto the ground, which also lit aflame as he fell to it.

"Lor! No!" Jasper shouted, running towards her with Emery behind.

"We have to. If there are two of us with this strength, we can kill him for sure. It feels amazing Jasper."

"Lor, we don't need to kill him. We don't need to hurt anyone!" Emery said, looking at her as Elias got up.

"Powerful isn't enough, is it Lor? Have you ever felt so powerful? That's the waitress's power running through your veins. Her flame entangled with your own." Elias said as he slowly stood back up.

Lor looked over at him and her flames grew bigger.

"Emery, I need you to go back to the car." Lor said, standing in front of Emery now.

"Imagine hers." Elias boomed, walking closer. "Imagine the power if you took hers." He said, pointing to Emery. "You could save them all. Live here in luxury. You would be in charge."

Emery thought she saw Lor's eyes becoming orange. Jasper put his hand on Emery.

"Lor go." Emery said calmly. Lor nodded and walked away towards the other flamethrowers, all running down the hill. Then she turned around and shot one more giant fire towards Elias, pushing him down again. Then she turned and closed her eyes and shot a massive stream of fire straight at Emery's heart.

Her closed eyes didn't account for love, though. She didn't account for Jasper knowing his sister as well as he did. He tried to push Emery out of the way. But Jasper didn't account for Emery, who lit up with fire so much that the power pushed Jasper down. The fire burned straight through Lor, and straight into Emery's body. Emery fell to the ground silently as Lor opened her eyes finally, to see Jasper holding Emery's body that was partially faded to ash.

Jasper let out a yell that sounded both weak and powerful at the same time. Elias laughed as he stood up and lit his arms back on fire. He formed a large ball of fire above his head and then collapsed as he was shot with a tranquilizer gun. Keepers started running from the bushes. Jasper looked up, "Cars now!" Most of the children and adults escaping were already gone and supporters remained slowly coming out to help Elias.

Jasper cried over Emery's body and whispered.

"Stay alive together. We just had one more fire." He cried and decided in the back of his mind. He would stay here. He would die here. As people from the diner exchanged fire with the people from Camp Carce. Phillip had run and told them, just as Emery had hoped.

Everything had gone just fine. And yet everything had gone incredibly wrong. Lor ran off into the woods in another direction at the sight of her brother's pain. She was easy to spot as her body shot flames from it as she ran. Emery whose body was not all the way burned, but becoming blacker by the moment, held Jasper's hand with the remaining hand that wasn't burned off. Her body slowly going from feeling hot to cold, as the flames and darts were exchanged above them.

Through tears she saw Amanda and another teen limp out of the diner. Some flamethrowers lit up fire in front of them, threatening them to return inside. Jasper gave Emery a final kiss, but there was no spark this time. She closed her eyes for the last time, and then got up. He wasn't living for himself anymore. He couldn't. Emery was him. That was the future he was fighting for and now it was gone. But he would still live for others. He threw a fireball at the line, preventing them from leaving, and helped carry the girl out. He created almost a bubble of fire around them as they ran through the battle and down the hill.

They got to the cars and jumped in and drove straight back to the cabin as the battle between His Place Diner and Camp Carce continued. Jasper cried silently the whole way back and no one else said a single word on the drive. When they got back to the cabin, they all piled into cars and followed Amanda as she found another empty cabin miles away where they couldn't be found.

17

Origin Stories

Emery's dads reminded the world what true strength looked like at her funeral. They held hands and tried to keep their pain from crying out and scaring all the children. Jasper observed them from a seat near the back in his all-black suit. He wanted to be more like them, more put together, more kind and accepting.

But Jasper couldn't help but feel like they still had each other. They had a hand to hold, and he didn't have anyone. Ironically, as he thought these thoughts, kids from the new center he was creating would walk by him and nod their heads in recognition and he would nod back.

For some reason, he couldn't stop looking at her dads the whole time. He felt like he needed to tell them something, but he wasn't sure what. Now that Emery was gone, it was almost like no one would ever know what they had. No one else but them shared those special moments, and something felt wrong about that. Some part of him wanted to stand on the bench he sat on and shout into the crowd that he loved Emery, and she loved him too. But he knew this door had closed for him.

Instead, he waited till everyone besides her dads had left. They sat at a bench in front of her coffin and stared. Jasper finally found the bravery and went to sit next to them.

"I'm Jasper. I was close with Emery."

Joaquin put his arm around him and pulled him in for the slightest hug.

"It's nice to meet you Jasper."

"I...I am so sorry." Jasper continued.

"She wouldn't want you to be."

"I know, but I just don't know what else to be."

"You could be strong."

Jasper sighed and looked at the coffin as he continued.

"I don't believe in angels."

Her dads looked at him with care and Jasper looked back at them.

"But I can't picture her as anything but."

They smiled, and a tear dropped down Joaquin's face.

"Do you think she is an angel?" Jasper asked.

"I can't imagine her as anything else."

"I can't help but feel guilty. It was my sister, you know." He said with his head as far down as possible and his eyes bearing into the ground with force.

"You can't hold that with you. Emery was a hero. But she could have been anything else. We are only responsible for ourselves." Joaquin said, giving Jasper l final pat on the back before grabbing Erick's hand and leaving.

Joaquin was right, of course, and Emery was a hero. But Jasper was right too, and his sister was ultimately a villain.

You really never know about people; they are too difficult to predict, and the real problem is that villains and heroes always have the same origin stories.

The Deepest Burn

CPSIA information can be obtained
at www.ICGtesting.com
Printed in the USA
BVHW041407170322
631760BV00016B/519